THE WILD BOYS

William S. Burroughs

THE WILD BOYS
A BOOK OF THE DEAD

GROVE PRESS □ New York

Grove Press
841 Broadway
New York, NY 10003

Acknowledgment is due to Alfred A. Knopf, Inc., for permission to quote from *The Trial* by Franz Kafka, translated by Willa and Edwin Muir, copyright 1937, © 1956 by Alfred A. Knopf, Inc. "Mother and I Would Like to Know" was first published in *Evergreen Review* No. 67; an earlier version appeared in *Mayfair* and was reprinted in *The Job*.

The Wild Boys appeared in the collection *The Soft Machine, Nova Express, and The Wild Boys: Three Novels,* published as a Black Cat Book in 1980 and an Evergreen Book in 1988.

Library of Congress Cataloging-in-Publication Data

Burroughs, William S., 1914–
 The wild boys : a book of the dead / William S. Burroughs. — 1st ed.
  p. cm.
 ISBN 0-8021-3331-2
 I. Title.
 PS3552.U75W485 1992
 813'.54—dc20   92-19273
                    CIP

Manufactured in the United States of America

First Edition 1971

First Black Cat Edition 1973

First Evergreen Edition 1992

CONTENTS

Tío Mate Smiles   3

The Chief Smiles   19

Old Sarge Smiles   25

And Bury the Bread Deep in a Sty   32

The Penny Arcade Peep Show   38

Le Gran Luxe   50

The Penny Arcade Peep Show   68

The Miracle of the Rose   71

A Silver Smile   82

The Frisco Kid 93

The Penny Arcade Peep Show 100

The Dead Child 102

"Just Call Me Joe" 121

"Mother and I Would Like to Know" 138

The Wild Boys 145

The Penny Arcade Peep Show 162

The Penny Arcade Peep Show 168

The Wild Boys Smile 172

THE WILD BOYS

Tío Mate Smiles

The camera is the eye of a cruising vulture flying over an area of scrub, rubble and unfinished buildings on the outskirts of Mexico City.

Five-story building no walls no stairs . . . squatters have set up makeshift houses . . . floors are connected by ladders . . . dogs bark, chickens cackle, a boy on the roof makes a jack-off gesture as the camera sails past.

Close to the ground we see the shadow of our wings, dry cellars choked with thistles, rusty iron rods sprouting like metal plants from cracked concrete, a broken bottle in the sun, shit-stained color comics, an Indian boy against a wall with his knees up eating an orange sprinkled with red pepper.

The camera zooms up past a red-brick tenement

studded with balconies where bright pimp shirts flutter purple, yellow, pink, like the banners of a medieval fortress. On these balconies we glimpse flowers, dogs, cats, chickens, a tethered goat, a monkey, an iguana. The *vecinos* lean over the balconies to exchange gossip, cooking oil, kerosene and sugar. It is an old folklore set played out year after year by substitute extras.

Camera sweeps to the top of the building where two balconies are outlined against the sky. The balconies are not exactly one over the other since the top balcony recedes a little. Here the camera stops . . . ON SET.

It is a bright windy morning China-blue half-moon in the sky. Joselito, the *maricón* son of Tía Dolores, has propped up a mirror by the rain barrel and is shaving the long silky black hairs from his chest in the morning wind while he sings

"NO PEGAN A MIO." ("DON'T HIT ME.")

It is an intolerable sound that sets spoons tinkling in saucers and windowpanes vibrating. The *vecinos* mutter sullenly.

"Es el puto que canta." ("It is the queer who sings.")
"The son of Dolores." She crosses herself.

A young man rolls off his wife despondently.
"No puedo con eso puto cantando." ("I can't do it with that queer singing.")
"The son of Dolores. She has the evil eye."

In each room the face of Joselito singing *"NO PEGAN A MIO"* is projected onto the wall.

Shot shows an old paralyzed man and Joselito's face inches from his screaming *"NO PEGAN A MIO."*
"Remember that he is the son of Dolores."
"And one of Lola's 'Little Kittens.' "

Tía Dolores is an old woman who runs a newspaper-and-tobacco kiosk. Clearly Joselito is her professional son.

On the top balcony is Esperanza just down from the mountains since her husband and all her brothers are in prison for growing opium poppies. She is a massive woman with arms like a wrestler and a permanent bucktoothed snarl. She leans over the balcony wall.

"Puto grosero, tus chingoa de pelos nos soplan en la cocina."

("Vulgar queer, your fucking hairs are blowing into our food.")

Shot shows hairs sprinkling soup and dusting an omelet like fine herbs.

The epithet *"grosero"* is too much for Joselito. He whirls cutting his chest. He clutches the wound with an expression of pathic dismay like a dying saint in an El Greco painting. He gasps *"MAMACITA"* and folds to the red tiles of the balcony dripping blood.

This brings Tía Dolores from her lair under the stairs, a rat's nest of old newspapers and magazines. Her evil eyes rotate in a complex calendar, and these calculations occupy her for many hours each night settled in her nest she puffs and chirps and twitters and writes in notebooks that are stacked around her bed with magazines on astrology . . . "Tomorrow my noon eye will be at its full." . . . This table of her power is so precise that she has to know the day hour minute and second to be sure of an ascendant eye and to this end she carries about with her an assortment of clocks, watches and sundials on thongs and chains. She can make her two eyes do different things, one spinning clockwise the other counterclockwise or she can pop one eye out onto her cheek laced with angry red veins while the other sinks back into an enigmatic grey slit. Latterly she has set up a schedule of *"ojos dulces"* ("sweet eyes") and gained some renown as a healer though Tío Mate says he would rather have ten of her evils than one of her sweets. But he is a bitter old man who lives in the past.

Dolores is a formidable war machine rather like a gun turret, dependent on split-second timing and the reflector disk of her kiosk, she is not well designed for surprise encounters.

Enter the American tourist. He thinks of himself as a good guy but when he looks in the mirror to shave this good guy he has to admit that "well, other people are different from me and I don't really like them." This makes him feel guilty toward other people. Tía Dolores hunches her cloak of malice closer and regards him with stony disapproval.

"Buenas días señorita."

"Desea algo?"

"Sí . . . Tribune . . Tribune Americano . . ."

Silently pursing her lips she folds the *Herald Tribune* and hands it to him. Trying not to watch what the woman is doing with her eyes, he fumbles for change. Suddenly his hand jumps out of the pocket scattering coins on the pavement. He stoops to pick them up.

A child hands him a coin.

"Gracias . . . Gracias."

The child looks at him with cold hatred. He stands there with the coins in his hand.

"Es cuanto?"

"Setenta centavos."

He hands her a peso. She drops it into a drawer and pushes the change at him.

"*Gracias . . . Gracias . . .*"

She stares at him icily. He stumbles away. Halfway down the block he screams out

"I'LL KILL THE OLD BITCH."

He begins to shadowbox and point pistols. People stop and stare.

Children scream after him.

"Son bitch Merican crazy man."

A policeman aproaches jerkily.

"*Señor oiga . . .*"

"OLD BITCH . . . OLD BITCH."

He lashes out wildly in a red haze blood cold on his shirt.

Enter a pregnant woman. She orders the Spanish edition of *Life*. Looking straight at the woman's stomach, Dolores' eyes glaze over and roll back in her head.

"*Nacido muerto*" ("Born dead") whispers Tío Pepe who has sidled up beside the woman.

On "sweet eye" days she changes her kiosk to a flower stall and sits there beaming the sweetest old flower lady of them all.

Enter the American tourist his face bandaged his arm in a sling.

"Ah! the American caballero wishes the *Tribune*. Today I sell flowers but this paper I have kept for you."

Her eyes crease in a smile that suffuses her face with gentle light.

"*Aquí señor, muchas gracias.*"

The paper smells faintly of roses. The coins leap into his hand.

Giving him the change she presses a coin into his palm and folds his fingers over it.

"This will bring you luck señor."

He walks down the street smiling at children who smile back . . . "I guess that's what we come here for . . . these children . . . that old flower lady back there . . ."

Enter the woman whose male child was born dead. She has come to buy a flower for his grave. Tía Dolores shakes her head sadly.

"*Pobrecito.*" ("Poor little one.")

The woman proffers a coin. Tía Dolores holds up her hands.

"*No señora . . . Es de mío . . .*"

However, her timing schedule necessitates a constant shift of props and character . . . "My sweet eye wanes with the moon" . . . That day the tourist reached his hotel in a state of collapse for a terrible street boy followed him from the kiosk screaming

"Son bitch puto queer, I catching one clap from fucky you asshole."

Sometimes half her booth is a kiosk and the other half a flower stall and she sits in the middle, her sweet eye on one side and her kiosk eye on the other. She can alternate sweet and evil twenty-four times a second her eyes jumping from one socket to the other.

Confident from her past victories, Tía Dolores waddles out onto the balcony like a fat old bird.

"*Pobrecito*" . . . She strokes Joselito's head gathering her powers.

"Tell your *maricón* son to shave in the house."

With a hasty glance at three watches, Dolores turns to

face this uncouth peasant woman who dares to challenge her dreaded eye.

"*Vieja loca, que haces con tu ojos?*" sneers Esperanza. "*Tu te pondrás ciego como eso.*" ("Old crazy one, what are you doing with your eyes? You will blind yourself doing that."

Dolores gasps out "TÍO PEPE" and sinks to the deck by her stricken son.

And Tío Pepe pops out tying his pants in front with a soggy length of grey rope. Under a travesty of good nature his soul is swept by raw winds of hate and mischance. He reads the newspapers carefully gloating over accidents, disasters and crime he thinks he is causing by his "*sugestiónes.*" His magic consists in whispering potent phrases from newspapers ". . . there are no survivors . . . condemned to death . . . fire of unknown origins . . . charred bodies . . ." This he does in crowds where people are distracted or better, much better right into the ear of someone who is sleeping or unconscious from drink. If no one is around and he is sure of his flop he reinforces his "*sugestiónes*" by thumping him in the testicles, grinding a knuckle into his eye or clapping cupped hands over his ears.

Here is a man asleep on a park bench. Tío Pepe approaches. He sits down by the man and opens a paper. He leans over reading into the man's ear, a thick slimy whisper.

"*No hay supervivientes.*" The man stirs uneasily. "*Muerto en el acto.*" The man shakes his head and opens his eyes. He looks suspiciously at Tío Pepe who has both hands on the paper. He stands up and taps his pockets. He walks away.

And there is a youth sleeping in a little park. Tío Pepe drops a coin by the boy's head. Bending down to pick up the coin he whispers . . . *"un joven muerto."* ("a dead youth.")

Several times the *vecinos* shoo him away from a sleeper and he hops away like an old vulture showing his yellow teeth in a desperate grin. Now he has picked up the spoor of drunken vomit and there is the doll sprawled against a wall, his pants streaked with urine. Bending down as if to help the man up, Tío Pepe whispers in both ears again and again . . . *"accidente horrible"* . . . He stands up and shrieks in a high falsetto voice . . . *"EMASCULADO EMASCULADO EMASCULADO"* and kicks the man three times gently in the groin.

He finds an old drunken woman sleeping in a pile of rags and claps a hand over her mouth and nose whispering . . . *"vieja borracha asfixiado."* ("old drunken woman asphyxiated.")

Another drunk is sleeping in dangerous proximity to a brush fire.

Tío Pepe drops a burning cigarette butt into the man's outstretched hand squatting down on his haunches he whispers slimily . . . *"cuerpo carbonizado . . . cuerpo carbonizado . . . cuerpo carbonizado. . . ."* He throws back his head and sings to the dry brush, the thistles the wind . . . *"cuerpo carbonizado . . . cuerpo carbonizado . . . cuerpo carbonizado . . ."*

He looks up at Esperanza with a horrible smile.

"Ah! the country cousin rises early." While he croons a little tune.

"*Resbalando sobre un pedazo de jabón*   Slipping on a piece of soap *se precipito de un balcón.*"   fell over a balcony.

Esperanza swings her great arm in a contemptuous arc and wraps a wet towel around the balcony wall spattering Tío Pepe, Dolores and Joselito with dirty water. Sneering over her shoulder she turns to go inside.

The beaten team on the lower balcony lick their wounds and plot revenge.

"If I can but get her in front of my kiosk at 9:23 next Thursday . . ."

"If I could find her *borracho* . . ."

"And I will have her gunned down by *pistoleros* . . ."

This boast of Joselito is predicated on his peculiar relationship with Lola La Chata. Lola La Chata is a solid 300 pounds cut from the same mountain rock as Esperanza. She sells heroin to pimps and thieves and whores and keeps the papers between her massive dugs.

Joselito had a junky boy friend who took him to meet Lola.

Joselito danced flamenco screeching like a peacock. Lola laughed and adopted him as one of her "Little Kittens." In a solemn ceremony he had suckled at her great purple dug bitter with heroin. It was not uncommon for Lola to service customers with two "Little Kittens" sucking at her breasts.

As Esperanza turns to go inside six pimpish young men burst through the door in a reek of brilliantine and lean over the balcony screaming insults at Joselito.

This brings reinforcements to the faltering lower balcony. Tío Mate stalks out followed by his adolescent Ka El Mono.

Tío Mate is an old assassin with twelve deer on his gun. A thin ghostly old man with eyes the color of a faded grey flannel shirt. He wears a black suit and a black Stetson. Under the coat a single action Smith & Wesson tip up forty-four with a seven-inch barrel is strapped to his lean flank. Tío Mate wants to put another deer on his gun before he dies.

The expression a "deer" (*un* "*venado*") derives from the mountainous districts of northern Mexico where the body is usually brought into the police post draped over a horse like a deer.

A young district attorney just up from the capital. Tío Mate has dropped by to give him a lesson in folklore.

Tío Mate (rolling a cigarette): "I'm going to send you a deer, *señor abogado.*"

The D.A. (he thinks "well now that's nice of him"): "Well thank you very much, if it isn't too much trouble . . ."

Tío Mate (lighting the cigarette and blowing out smoke): "No trouble at all *señor abogado*. It is my pleasure."

Tío Mate blows smoke from the muzzle of his forty-four and smiles.

Man is brought in draped over a saddle. The horse is led by a woodenfaced Indian cop. The D.A. comes out. The cop jerks his head back . . . "*un venado.*"

Tío Mate had been the family *pistolero* of rich landowners in northern Mexico. The family was ruined by expropriations when they backed the wrong presidential candidate and Tío Mate came to live with relatives

in the capital. His room is a bare, white cell, a cot, a
trunk, a little wooden case in which he keeps his charts,
sextant and compass. Every night he cleans and oils his
forty-four. It is a beautiful custom-made gun given to
him by the *patrón* for killing "my unfortunate brother
the General." It is nickel-plated and there are hunting
scenes engraved on the cylinder and barrel. The handles
are of white porcelain with two blue deer heads. There
is nothing for Tío Mate to do except oil his gun and
wait. The gun glints in his eyes a remote mineral calm.
He sits for hours on the balcony with his charts and in-
struments spread out on a green felt card table. Only
his eyes move as he traces vultures in the sky. Occasionally he draws a line on the chart or writes down
numbers in a logbook. Every Independence Day the
vecinos assemble to watch Tío Mate blast a vulture
from the sky with his forty-four. Tío Mate consults his
charts and picks a vulture. His head moves very slightly
from side to side eyes on the distant target he draws
aims and fires: a vulture trailing black feathers down
the sky. So precise are Tío Mate's calculations that one
feather drifts down on to the balcony. This feather is
brought to Tío Mate by El Mono his Feather Bearer.
Tío Mate puts the feather in his hat band. There are
fifteen black years in his band.

El Mono has been Tío Mate's Feather Bearer for five
years. He sits for hours on the balcony until their faces
fuse. He has his own little charts and compass. He is
learning to shoot a vulture from the sky. A thin agile boy
of thirteen he climbs all over the building spying on the
vecinos. He wears a little blue skullcap and when he
takes it off the *vecinos* hurry to drop a coin in it. Other-
wise he will act out a recent impotence, a difficult bowel

movement, a cunt-licking with such precise mimicry that anyone can identify the party involved.

El Mono picks out a pimp with his eyes. He makes a motion of greasing a candle. The pimp licks his lips speechless with horror his eyes wild. Now El Mono is shoving the candle in and out his ass teeth bare eyes rolling he gasps out: *"Sangre de Cristo . . ."* The pimp impaled there for all to see. Joselito leaps up and stomps out a triumphant fandango. Awed by Tío Mate and fearful of a recent impotence, a difficult bowel movement, a cunt-licking, the pimps fall back in confusion.

Tío Paco now mans the upper balcony with his comrade in arms Fernández the drug clerk. Tío Paco has been a waiter for forty years. Very poor, very proud, contemptuous of tips, he cares only for the game. He brings the wrong order and blames the client, he flicks the nastiest towel, he shoves a tip back saying "The house pays us." He screams after a client *"Le service n'est-ce pas compris."* He has studied with Pullman George and learned the art of jiggling arms across the room:

hot coffee in a quiet American crotch.

And woe to a waiter who crosses him:

tray flies into the air. Rich well-dressed clients dodge cups and glasses, bottle of Fundador broken on the floor.

Fernández hates adolescents, pop stars, beatniks, tourists, queers, criminals, tramps, whores and drug addicts. Tío Paco hates their type too.

Fernández likes policemen, priests, army officers, rich people of good repute. Tío Paco likes them too. He serves them quickly and well. But their lives must be above reproach.

A newspaper scandal can mean long waits for service.

The client becomes impatient. He makes an angry gesture. A soda siphon crashes to the floor.

What they both love most of all is to inflict humiliation on a member of the hated classes, and to give information to the police.

Fernández throws a morphine script back across the counter.

"*No prestamos servicio a los viciosos.*" ("We do not serve dope fiends.")

Tío Paco ignores a pop star and his common-law wife until the cold sour message seeps into their souls:

"We don't want your type in here."

Fernández holds a prescription in his hand. He is a plump man in his late thirties. Behind dark glasses his eyes are yellow and liverish. His low urgent voice on the phone.

"*Receta narcótica falsificado.*" ("A narcotic prescription forged.")

"Your prescription will be ready in a minute *señor.*"

Tío Paco stops to wipe a table and whispers . . . "Marijuana in a suitcase . . . table by the door" . . . The cop pats his hand.

Neither Tío Paco nor Fernández will accept any reward for services rendered to their good friends the police.

When they first came to live on the top floor five years ago Tío Mate saw them once in the hall.

"Copper-loving bastards," he said in his calm final voice.

He did not have occasion to look at them again. Anyone Tío Mate doesn't like soon learns to stay out of Tío Mate's space.

Fernández steps to the wall and his wife appears at his side. Her eyes are yellow her teeth are gold. Now his daughter appears. She has a mustache and hairy legs. Fernández looks down from a family portrait.

"*Criminales. Maricónes. Vagabundos.* I will denounce you to the police."

Tío Paco gathers all the bitter old men in a blast of sour joyless hate. Joselito stops dancing and droops like a wilted flower. Tío Pepe and Dolores are lesser demons. They shrink back furtive and timorous as dawn rats. Tío Mate looks at a distant point beyond the old waiter tracing vultures in the sky. El Mono stands blank and cold. He will not imitate Fernández and Tío Paco.

And now Tía María, retired fat lady from a traveling carnival, comes out onto the lower balcony supporting her vast weight on two canes. Tía María eats candy and reads love stories all day and gives card readings the cards sticky and smudged with chocolate. She secretes a heavy sweetness. Sad and implacable it flows out of her like a foam runway. The *vecinos* fear her sweetness which they regard fatalistically as a natural hazard like earthquakes and volcanoes. "The Sugar of Mary" they call it. It could get loose one day and turn the city into a cake.

She looks up at Fernández and her sad brown eyes pelt him with chocolates. Tío Paco tries desperately to outflank her but she sprays him with maraschino cherries from her dugs and coats him in pink icing. Tío Paco is the little man on a wedding cake all made out of candy. She will eat him later.

Now Tío Gordo, the blind lottery-ticket seller, rolls his immense bulk out onto the upper balcony, his wheel chair a chariot, his snarling black dog at his side. The dog smells all the money Tío Gordo takes. A torn note brings an ominous growl, a counterfeit and it will break the man's arm in its powerful jaws, brace its legs and hold him for the police. The dog leaps to the balcony wall and hooks its paws over barking, snarling, bristling, eyes phosphorescent. Tía María gasps and the sugar runs out of her. She is terrified of "rage dogs" as she calls them. The dog seems ready to leap down onto the lower balcony. Tío Mate plots the trajectory its body would take. He will kill it in the air.

Tío Pepe throws back his head and howls:

"*Perro attropellado para un camión.*" ("Dog run over by a truck.")

The dog drags its broken hindquarters in a dusty noon street.

The dog slinks whimpering to Tío Gordo.

González the Agente wakes up muttering "*Chingoa*" the fumes of Mescal burning in his brain. Buttoning on his police tunic and forty-five he pushes roughly to the wall of the upper balcony.

González is a broken dishonored man. All the *vecinos* know he has much fear of Tío Mate and crosses the street to avoid him. El Mono has acted out both parts.

González looks down and there is Tío Mate waiting. The hairs stand up straight on González's head.

"CHINGOA."

He snatches out his forty-five and fires twice. The bullets whistle past Tío Mate's head. Tío Mate smiles. In one smooth movement he draws aims and fires. The heavy slug catches González in his open mouth ranging up through the roof blows a large tuft of erect hairs out the back of González's head. González folds across the balcony wall. The hairs go limp and hang down from his head. The balcony wall begins to sway like a horse. His forty-five drops to the lower balcony and goes off.

Shot breaks the camera. A frozen still of the two balconies tilted down at a forty-five-degree angle. González still draped over the wall sliding forward, the wheel chair halfway down the upper balcony, the dog slipping down on braced legs, the *vecinos* trying to climb up and slipping down.

"GIVE ME THE SIXTEEN."

The cameraman shoots wildly . . . pimps scream by teeth bare eyes rolling, Esperanza sneers down at the Mexican earth, the fat lady drops straight down her pink skirts billowing up around her, Tía Dolores sails down her eyes winking sweet and evil like a doll, dog falls across a gleaming empty sky.

The camera dips and whirls and glides tracing vultures higher and higher spiraling up.

Last take: Against the icy blackness of space ghost faces of Tío Mate and El Mono. Dim jerky faraway stars splash the cheek bones with silver ash. *Tío Mate smiles.*

The Chief Smiles

Marrakech 1976 . . . Arab house in the Medina charming old pot-smoking Fatima drinking tea with the trade in the kitchen. Here in the middle of a film to find myself one of the actors. The Chief has asked me to his house for dinner.

"Around Eight Rogers."

He received me in his patio mixing a green salad thick steaks laid out by the barbecue pit.

"Help yourself to a drink Rogers." He gestures to the drink wagon.
"There's kif of course if you want it."
I mixed myself a short drink and declined the kif.
"It gives me a headache."
I'd seen the Chief smoking with his Arab contacts but

that didn't give me a license to smoke. Besides it does give me a headache.

The Chief's cover story is an eccentric old French *comte* who is translating the Koran into Provencal and sometimes he will pull cover and bore his guests cata-tonic. You see, he really knows Provençal and Arabic. You have to study for years on a real undercover job like this. The Chief wasn't pulling cover tonight. He was expansive and "watch your step, Rogers" I told myself, sipping a weak Scotch.

" 'I think you are the man for a highly important and I may add highly dangerous assignment, Rogers.' You fell for that crap?"

"Well sir he is impressive," I said cautiously.

"He's a cheap old ham," said the Chief. He sat down and filled his kif pipe with one hand. He smoked and blew the ash out absently caressing a gazelle that nuzzled his knee.

" 'Gotta stay ahead of the Commies or everybody's kids will be learning Chinese.' What a windbag."

I endeavored to look noncommittal.

"Have you any idea what we're doing here, Rogers?"

"Well, no sir."

"I thought not. Never tell them what you want until you've got them where you want them. I'm going to show you a documentary film."

Two Arab servants carry out a six-foot screen and set it up ten feet in front of our chairs. The Chief gets up turning switches adjusting dials.

A jungle seen through a faceted eye that looks simul-taneously in any direction up or down . . . close-up of a green snake with golden eyes . . . telescopic lens picks out a monkey caught by an eagle between two vast

trees. The monkey is borne away screaming. I can feel
a probing insect intelligence behind the camera, pyramids ahead fields and huts. In the fields workers are
planting maize seeds under the direction of an overseer
with staff and headdress. Close-up of a worker's face.
Whatever it is that makes a man a man, all feeling and
all soul has gone out in that face. Nothing is left but
body needs and body pleasures. I have seen faces like
that in the back wards of state hospitals for the insane.
Faces that live to eat, shit and masturbate. Satisfied
with the inspection the camera moves back to observe
group patterns of the workers. They are moving
through a three-dimensional film of the operation that
covers them with a grey sheen. Occasionally the overseer adjusts a slow worker with his eyes.

Next take shows a room in the temple suffused with
underwater light. An old priest naked to his pendulous
dugs and atrophied testicles sits cross-legged on a toilet
seat set in the floor. The seat is cushioned with human
skin on which are tattooed pictures of a man turning
into a giant centipede. The centipede is eating him
from inside legs and claws grow through screaming
flesh. Now the centipede is eating his screaming mouth.

"Criminals and captives sentenced to death in centipede are tattooed with those pictures on every inch of
their bodies. They are left for three days to fester. Then
they are brought out given a powerful aphrodisiac,
skinned alive in orgasm and strapped into a segmented
copper centipede. The centipede is placed with obscene
endearments in a bed of white-hot coals. The priests
gather in crab suits and eat the meat out of the shell
with gold claws."
The old priest looks like a living part in an exotic com-

puter. From festering sockets in his spine fine copper wires trail in a delicate fan. The camera follows the wires. Here in a little copper cage a scorpion is eating her mate. Here the head of a captive protrudes through the floor. Red ants have made a hill in his head. They crawl in and out of empty eye sockets. They have eaten his lips away from a gag. A muffled scream without a tongue torn through his perforated palate showers the floor with bloody ants. In jade aquariums human rectums and genitals grafted onto other flesh . . . a prostate gland quivers rainbow colors through a pink mollusk . . . two translucent white salamanders squirm in slow sodomy golden eyes glinting enigmatic lust . . . Lesbian electric eels squirm on a mud flat crackling their vaginas together . . . erect nipples sprout from a bulbous plant.

"They know an aphrodisiac so potent that it shatters the body to quivering pieces. The Sweet Death is reserved for comely youths and maidens. This wonderful old people had a rich folklore. Well I happened onto this good thing through a Mexican shoe-shine boy . . . Yoo-hoo Kiki. . . Come out and show Mr. Rogers how pretty you are . . ."

Kiki stands in a doorway smiling like a shy young animal.
"Now that lad . . . he's a doll isn't he? . . . is one of the best deep trance mediums I have ever handled. Through him I was able to teleport myself to a Mayan set and bring back the pictures. The whole thing was so frantic I cooled it all the way in my reports. All I said was it looks like a lovely WUP. That's code for Weapon of Unlimited Potential . . . He's hotting up now."

The old priest rocks back and forth. The wires stand up on his spine and his eyes light up inside. His lips part and a dry insect music buzzes out.

"It's known as singing the pictures. The principle is alternating current. That old fuck can alternate pain and pleasure on a subvocal perhaps even a molecular level twenty-four times a second goading the natives around on stock probes in out up down here there into the prearranged molds laid down in the sacred books. A few singers can deliver direct current and they are only called in an emergency. The control system you have just seen broke down. This happened quite suddenly a whole generation was born that felt neither pain nor pleasure. There were no soldiers to bring captives from other tribes since soldiers would have endangered the control machine. They relied entirely on local criminals for the pain and pleasure pictures. As a last resort they called in the Incomparable Yellow Serpent."

The Serpent is carried in on his amber throne blue snake eyes skin like yellow parchment two long serpent fangs grafted into the upper jaw. As the current pulses through him he begins to rock back and forth. He shifts from A.C. to D.C. A thin siren wail breaks from his lips now open to the yellow fangs.
DEATH DEATH DEATH
The pictures crash and leap from his eyes blasting worker and priest alike to smoldering fragments.
DEATH DEATH DEATH
A thin siren wail rises and falls over empty cities.

"This secret of the ancient Mayans which few are competent to practice.
When comes such another singer as the Old Yellow Serpent?"

"Now the Technical Department think we are all as crazy as our way of life is reprehensible.

" 'Bring us the ones that work' they say 'facts, figures, personnel.

" 'Put that joker DEATH on the line. Take care of Mao and his gang of cutthroats.'

"I was privileged to assist in a manner of speaking at the Yellow Serpent's last broadcast in Washington D.C."

Room in the Pentagon. Generals, CIA, State Department fidget about with that top secret hottest thing ever look open line to the President Strategic and NATO standing by. The Old Yellow Serpent is carried in by four marine guards. He begins to rock back and forth. He breathes in baby coos and breathes out death rattles. He sucks in wheat fields and spits out dust bowls.

"He's just warming up," says the CIA man to a five-star general.

The Old Serpent shifts to D.C. blazing like a comet.

DEATH DEATH DEATH

The pictures lash and crackle from his eyes.

DEATH DEATH DEATH

A wall blows out and spills screaming brass eighteen floors to the street.

DEATH DEATH DEATH

And now the Serpent swings his whip in the sky.

Here lived stupid vulgar sons of bitches who thought they could hire DEATH as a company cop . . . empty streets, old newspapers in the wind, a rustle of darkness and wires.

In the night sky over St Louis the Mayan Death God does a Cossack dance shooting stars from his eyes. *The Chief smiles.*

Old
Sarge
Smiles

The Green Nun has stopped the unfortunate traveler in front of her red-brick priory set among oak trees, green lawns and flower beds.

"Oh do come in and see my mental ward and the wonderful things we are doing for the patients."

She walks with him up the gravel drive to the priory door pointing to her flowers.

"Aren't my primroses doing nicely."

She opens the door of the priory with a heavy brass key at her belt. Down a long hall and flight of stairs she opens another door with her keys. She shows Audrey into a bare cold ward room crayon drawings on the wall. A nun walks up and down with a ruler. The patients are busy with plasticene and crayons. It looks like a kindergarten but some of the children are middle-aged. The door clicks shut and her voice changes.

"You'll find plasticene and crayons over there. You must have permission to leave the room for any purpose."

"Now see here . . ."

A paunchy guard with a tin helmet and wide leather belt stands beside her. The guard looks at him with cold ugly hate and says:

"He wants Bob and his lawyers."

At six o'clock there is a tasteless dinner of cold macaroni that Audrey does not touch. After dinner the night sister comes on.

Cots are set up by the patients and the ward room is converted into a dormitory.

"Anyone want potty before lights out?"

She jangles the keys. The lavatory cubicles stand at one end of the dormitory. The sister on duty unlocks the doors and stands in the open door watching coldly.

"Now don't try and play with your dirty thing again Coldcliff or you'll have six hours in the kitchen."

A dim religious light burns all night in the dormitory. The patients sleep on their backs under a thin blanket. Erections are sanctioned with a sharp ruler tap from the night sister.

And so the years passed. Sometimes as a special treat there were nature walks in the garden, Bob there with three snarling Alsatians on a lead. The patients could watch a praying mantis eat her mate.

Daily confessions were heard by the Green Nun on a lie detector that could also give a very nasty shock in the nasty places while the Green Nun intoned slowly "Thou shalt not bear false witness."

These confessions she wrote out in green ink keeping a separate ledger book for each patient. Once after a particularly degraded confession she levitated to the ceiling in the presence of an awed young nun. Every night she put on Christ drag with a shimmering halo and visited some young nun in her cell. She liked to think of herself as the nun in a poem by Sara Teasdale.

"Infinite tenderness infinite irony is hidden forever in her closed eyes.

Who must have learned too well in her long loneliness how empty wisdom is even to the wise."

She was an inveterate hypochondriac and dosed herself liberally with laudanum. As a result she suffered from constipation which could put a comely young nun on high colonic duty. This honor was invariably followed by a nocturnal visit from Christ with a strap-on. In her youth the Green Nun had toyed with the idea of ordering Bob to raid a sperm bank. Then she could claim the Christ child. She put aside these ambitious thoughts. Her work in the kindergarten was more important than worldly glamor, her picture on the cover of *Life*.

You learn not to have a thought you will be ashamed to tell the Green Nun and never to do anything you would be ashamed to do in front of her. And sooner or later you join the Quarter G Club. Converted patients are allowed a quarter grain of morphine every night before lights out, a privilege which is withdrawn for any trespass.

"Now you know that dream about flying is WRONG don't you? For that you go to bed without your medicine."

Shivering with junk sickness in the icy ward room all next day he has to look bright and happy as he busies himself with crayons and plasticene. He has learned to draw pictures of the Virgin Mary and Saint Teresa with an unmistakable resemblance to the Green Nun. Crosses are always safe in plasticene. Soon after his commitment he made the error of molding a naked Greek statue. That day sister's ruler slashed down on his thin blue wrist and he was forced to write out *i am a filthy little beast* ten thousand times in many places.

Dizzy dance of rooms and faces, murmur of many voices smell of human nights . . . St. Louis backdrop of red-brick houses, slate roofs, back yards and ash pits . . . As a child he had an English governess with references so impeccable that Audrey later suspected they had been forged by a Fleet Street hack in a shabby pub near Earl's Court.

"You can't put in too many Lords and Lydies I always sy."

Listening back with a writer's crystal set he picked up mutters of the servant underworld . . . the pimping blackmailing chauffeur . . . "You don't get rid of me that easy Lord Brambletie."

Overdose of morphine in a Kensington nursing home . . . "She said that Mrs. Charrington was sleeping and could not be disturbed."

The governess left quite suddenly after receiving a letter from England.

Then there was an old Irish crone who taught him to call the toads. She could go out into the back yard and croon a toad out from under a stone and Audrey learned to do it too. He had his familiar toad that lived under a rock by the goldfish pool and came when he called it. And she taught him a curse to bring "the blinding worm" from rotten bread.

Audrey went to a progressive grade school where the children were encouraged to express themselves, model in clay, beat out copper ash trays and make stone axes. A sensitive inspirational teacher is writing the school play out on the blackboard as the class makes suggestions:

ACT 1

SCENE ONE: *Two women at the water hole.*

Woman 1: "I hear the tiger ate Bast's baby last night."

Woman 2: "Yes. All they found was the child's toy soldier."

Woman 1: "One doesn't feel safe with that tiger about." (*She looks around nervously.*) "It's getting dark Sextet and I'm going home."

One of the truly great bores of St Louis was Colonel Greenfield. He had dinner jokes that took half an hour to tell during which no one was expected to eat. Audrey sits there watching his turkey go cold with half a mind to put the "blinding worm" on him. It seems this old black Jew has crashed the Palace Hotel in Palm Beach. At that very moment the night clerk, a new man just in from a Texas hotel school, withers in Major Brady's cold glare.

"Did you check in Mr Rogers nee Kike?"
"Why, yes sir, I did. He had a reservation."
"No, he didn't. There was a mistake you dumb hick. Don't you know a black Jew when you see one?"

Meanwhile the old black Jew has called room service
. . . "Will you please send up a little pepper."
"I'm sorry sir the kitchen is closed. Why it's three in
the morning."
"I don't care is the kitchen closed. I don't care is it three
in the morning. I want a little pepper."
"I'm sorry sir."
"I vant to talk with the manager plis" . . . (The dialect
gets heavier as the Colonel warms up.)
Call from the night manager to Major Brady's office . . .
"That old black Jew in 23 wants pepper of all things at
this hour."
"All right. We run a first-class hotel here. Open the
kitchen and give him anything he wants . . . Brought
his own carp most likely."
So the night manager calls the old black Jew. "All right
sir what kind of pepper do you want? Red pepper?
White pepper? Black pepper?"
"I don't vant red pepper. I don't vant white pepper. I
don't vant black pepper. All I vant is a little toilet
pepper."

eye in needle needle in eye

The Colonel burned down St Louis. One day when
Audrey reluctantly visited Colonel Greenfield's house
to deliver a message he found the Colonel telling his
interminable anecdotes to the Negro butler.
"Now on the old Greenfield plantation we had house
niggers and field niggers and the field niggers never
came into the house."
"No sir the field niggers never came into the house."
"The house niggers saw to that didn't they George?"
"Yes sir. The house niggers saw to that sir."
"Now wherever I go I always get out the telephone

book and look up anybody who bears the name of Greenfield. There are so few of them and they are all so distinguished. Well some years ago in Buffalo New York I had written down the address of Abraham L. Greenfield and showed it to a nigra cab driver."

"I think you got the wrong number boss."

"The address is correct driver."

"I still think you got the wrong number boss."

"Shut your black face and take me where I want to go."

"Yahsuh boss. Here you are boss. Niggertown boss."

"And that's where we were right in Niggertown."

"Yes sir. Right in Niggertown sir."

"So I get out and knock on the door and an old coon comes to the door with his hat in his hands."

"With his hat in his hands sir."

"Good evening Massa and God bless you" he says.

"Is your name Greenfield?" I ask him.

"Yahsuh boss. Abraham Lincoln Greenfield."

"Well it turns out he was one of our old house niggers."

"One of your old house niggers sir."

"He invited me in and served me a cup of coffee with homemade caramel cake. He wouldn't sit down just stood there nodding and smiling . . . The right kind of darky."

"The right kind of darky sir."

And Bury
the Bread
Deep
in a Sty

Audrey was a thin pale boy his face scarred by festering spiritual wounds. "He looks like a sheep-killing dog," said a St Louis aristocrat. There was something rotten and unclean about Audrey, an odor of the walking dead. Doormen stopped him when he visited his rich friends. Shopkeepers pushed his change back without a thank you. He spent sleepless nights weeping into his pillow from impotent rage. He read adventure stories and saw himself as a gentleman adventurer like the "Major" . . . sun helmet, khakis, Webley at the belt a faithful Zulu servant at his side. A dim sad child breathing old pulp magazines. At sixteen he attended an exclusive high school known as The Poindexter Academy where he felt rather like a precarious house nigger.

Still he was invited to most of the parties and Mrs Kindheart made a point of being nice to him.

At the opening of the academy in September a new boy appeared. Aloof and mysterious where he came from nobody knew. There were rumors of Paris, London, a school in Switzerland. His name was John Hamlin and he stayed with relatives in Portland Place. He drove a magnificent Dusenberg. Audrey, who drove a battered Moon, studied this vast artifact with openmouthed awe, the luxurious leather upholstery, the brass fittings, the wickerwork doors, the huge spotlight with a pistol-grip handle. Audrey wrote: "Clearly he has come a long way travel stained and even the stains unfamiliar, cuff links of a dull metal that seems to absorb light, his red hair touched with gold, large green eyes well apart."

The new boy took a liking to Audrey while he turned aside with polished deftness invitations from sons of the rich. This did not endear Audrey to important boys and he found his stories coldly rejected by the school magazine.

"Morbid" the editor told him. "We want stories that make you go to bed feeling good."

It was Friday October 23, 1929 a bright blue day leaves falling, half-moon in the sky. Audrey Carsons walked up Pershing Avenue . . . "*Simon, aime tu le bruit des pas sur les feuilles mortes?*" . . . He had read that on one of E. Holdeman Julius's little Blue Books and meant to use it in the story he was writing. Of course his hero spoke French. At the corner of Pershing and Walton he stopped to watch a squirrel. A dead leaf caught for a moment in Audrey's ruffled brown hair.

"Hello Audrey. Like to go for a ride?"

It was John Hamlin at the wheel of his Dusenberg. He opened the door without waiting for an answer. Hamlin made a wide U-turn and headed West . . . left on Euclid right on Lindell . . . Skinker Boulevard City Limits . . . Clayton . . . Hamlin looked at his wrist watch.

"We could make St Joseph for lunch . . . nice riverside restaurant there serves wine."

Audrey is thrilled of course. The autumn countryside flashes by . . . long straight stretch of road ahead.

"Now I'll show you what this job can do."

Hamlin presses the accelerator slowly to the floor . . . 60 . . . 70 . . . 80 . . . 85 . . . 90 . . . Audrey leans forward lips parted eyes shining.

At Tent City a top-level conference is in progress involving top level executives in the CONTROL GAME. The Conference has been called by a Texas billionaire who contributes heavily to MRA and maintains a stable of evangelists. This conference is taking place outside St Louis Missouri because the Green Nun flatly refuses to leave her kindergarten. The high teacup queens thought it would be fun to do a tent city like a 1917 Army camp. The conferents are discussing Operation W.O.G. (Wrath of God).

At the top level people get cynical after a few drinks. The young man from the news magazine has discovered a good-looking Fulbright scholar and they are witty in a corner over Martinis. A drunken American Sergeant reels to his feet. He has the close-cropped iron-grey hair and ruddy complexion of the Regular Army man.

"To put it country simple for a lay audience . . . you don't even know what buttons to push . . . we take a

bunch of longhair boys fucking each other while they puff reefers, spit cocaine on the Bible, and wipe their asses with Old Glory. We show this film to decent, church-going, Bible Belt do-rights. We take the reaction. One religious sheriff with seven nigger notches on his gun melted the camera lens. He turned out to be quite an old character and the boys from *Life* did a spread on him—seems it had always been in the family, a power put there by God to smite the unrighteous: his grandmother struck a whore dead in the street with it. When we showed the picture to a fat Southern senator his eyes popped out throwing fluid all over your photographer. Well I've been asparagrassed in Paris, kneed in the groin by the Sea Org in Tunis, maced in Chicago and pelted with scorpions in Marrakech so a face full of frog eggs is all in the day's work. What the Narco boys call 'society's disapproval' reflected and concentrated twenty million I HATE YOU pictures in one blast. When you want the job done come to the UNITED STATES OF AMERICA. AND WE CAN TURN IT IN ANY DIREC-TION. You Limey leftovers . . ." He points to a battery of old grey men in club chairs frozen in stony disapproval of this vulgar drunken American. When will the club steward arrive to eject the bounder so a gentleman can read his *Times?*
"YOU'RE NOTHING BUT A BANANA REPUBLIC. AND REMEMBER WE'VE GOT YOUR PICTURES."
"And we've got yours too Yank," they clip icily.
"MINE ARE UGLIER THAN YOURS."
The English cough and look away fading into their spectral clubs, yellowing tusks of the beast killed by the improbable hyphenated name, OLD SARGE screams after them . . . "WHAT DO YOU THINK THIS IS A BEAUTY CONTEST? You Fabian Socialist vegetable

peoples go back to your garden in Hampstead and re-
lease a hot-air balloon in defiance of a local ordinance
delightful encounter with the bobby in the morning.
Mums wrote it all up in her diary and read it to us at
tea. WE GOT ALL YOUR PANSY PICTURES AT
ETON. YOU WANTA JACK OFF IN FRONT OF
THE QUEEN WITH A CANDLE UP YOUR ASS?"
"You can't talk like that in front of decent women,"
drawled the Texas billionaire flanked by his rangers.
"You decorticated cactus. I suppose you think this con-
ference was your idea? Compliments of SID in the
Sudden Inspiration Department . . . And you lousy
yacking fink queens my photographers wouldn't take
your pictures. You are nothing but tape recorders. With
just a flick of my finger frozen forever over that Martini.
All right get snide and snippy about that HUH? . . .
And you" . . . He points to the Green Nun . . . "Write
out ten thousand times under water in indelible ink
OLD SARGE HAS MY CHRIST PICTURES. SHALL
I SHOW THEM TO THE POPE?

"And now in the name of all good tech sergeants everywhere . . ."

A gawky young sergeant is reading *Amazing Stories*.
He flicks a switch . . . Audrey and Hamlin on screen.
Wind ruffles Audrey's hair as the Dusenberg gathers
speed.
"Light Years calling Bicarbonate . . . Operation Little
Audrey on target . . . eight seconds to count down . . .
tracking . . ."

A thin dyspeptic technician mixes a bicarbonate of
soda.
"URP calling Fox Trot . . . six seconds to count
down . . ."

English computer programer is rolling a joint.

"Spot Light calling Accent . . . four seconds to count down . . ."

Computers hum, lights flash, lines converge.

Red-haired boy chews gum and looks at a muscle magazine.

"Red Dot calling Pin Point . . . two seconds to count down . . ."

The Dusenberg zooms over a rise and leaves the ground. Just ahead is a wooden barrier, steamroller, piles of gravel, phantom tents. DETOUR sign points sharp left to a red clay road where pieces of flint glitter in the sunlight.

"OLD SARGE IS TAKING OVER."

He looks around and the crockery flies off every table spattering the conferents with Martinis, bourbon, whipped cream, maraschino cherries, gravy and vichysoisse frozen forever in a 1920 slapstick.

"COUNT DOWN."

End over end a flaming pin wheel of jagged metal slices through the conferents. The Green Nun is decapitated by a twisted fender. The Texas billionaire is sloshed with gasoline like a burning nigger. The broken spotlight trailing white-hot wires like a jellyfish hits the British delegate in the face. The Dusenberg explodes throwing white-hot chunks of jagged metal, boiling acid, burning gasoline in all directions.

Wearing the uniforms of World War I Audrey and Old Sarge lean out of a battered Moon in the morning sky and smile. Old Sarge is at the wheel.

The
Penny Arcade
Peep Show

Unexpected rising of the curtain can begin with a Dusenberg moving slowly along a 1920 detour. Just ahead Audrey sees booths and fountains and ferris wheels against a yellow sky. A boy steps in front of the car and holds up his hand. He is naked except for a rainbow colored jock strap and sandals. Under one arm he carries a Mauser pistol clipped onto a rifle stock. He steps to the side of the car. Audrey has never seen anyone so cool and disengaged. He looks at Audrey and he looks at John. He nods.

"We leave the car here," John says. Audrey gets out. Six boys now stand there watching him serenely. They carry long knives sheathed at their belts which are studded with amethyst crystals. They all wear rainbow-colored jock straps like souvenir post cards of Niagara

Falls. Audrey follows John through a square where acts
are in progress surrounded by circles of adolescent onlookers eating colored ices and chewing gum. Most of
the boys wear the rainbow jock straps and a few of them
seem to be completely naked. Audrey can't be sure
trying to keep up with John. The fair reminds Audrey
of 1890 prints. Sepia ferris wheels turn in yellow light.
Gliders launched from a wooden ramp soar over the fair
ground legs of the pilots dangling in air. A colored
hot-air balloon is released to applause of the onlookers.
Around the fair ground are boardwalks, lodging houses,
restaurants and baths. Boys lounge in doorways. Audrey
glimpses scenes that quicken his breath and send the
blood pounding to his groin. He catches sight of John
far ahead outlined in the dying sunlight. Audrey calls
after him but his voice is blurred and muffled. Then
darkness falls as if someone has turned out the sky.
Some distance ahead and to the left he sees PENNY
ARCADE spelled out in light globes. Perhaps John has
gone in there. Audrey pushes aside a red curtain and
enters the arcade. Chandeliers, gilt walls, red curtains,
mirrors, windows stretch away into the distance. He
cannot see the end of it in either direction from the
entrance. It is a long narrow building like a ship cabin
or a train. Boys are standing in front of peep shows
some wearing the rainbow jock straps others in prep
school clothes loincloths and jellabas. He notices shows
with seats in front of them and some in curtained
booths. As he passes a booth he glimpses through parted
curtains two boys sitting on a silk sofa both of them
naked. Shifting his eyes he sees a boy slip his jock strap
down and step out of it without taking his eyes from
the peep show. Moving with a precision and ease he
sometimes knew in flying dreams Audrey slides onto a

steel chair that reminds him of Doctor Moor's Surgery in the Lister Building afternoon light through green blinds. In front of him is a luminous screen. Smell of old pain, ether, bandages, sick fear in the waiting room, yes this is Doctor Moor's Surgery in the Lister Building.

The doctor was a Southern gentleman of the old school. Rather like John Barrymore in appearance and manner he fancied himself as a witty raconteur which at times he was. The doctor had charm which Audrey so sadly lacked. No doorman would ever stop him no shopkeeper forget his thank you under eyes that could suddenly go cold as ice. It was impossible for the doctor to like Audrey. "He looks like a homosexual sheep-killing dog" he thought but he did not say this. He looked up from his paper in his dim gloomy drawing room and pontificated "the child is not wholesome."

His wife went further: "It is a walking corpse," she said. Audrey was inclined to agree with her but he didn't know whose corpse he was. And he was painfully aware of being unwholesome.

There is a screen directly in front of him, a screen to his left, a screen to his right, and a screen in back of his head. He can see all four screens from a point above his head.

Later Audrey wrote these notes: "The scenes presented and the manner of presentation varies according to an underlying pattern.

"1. Objects and scenes move away and come in with a slow hydraulic movement always at the same speed. The screens are three-dimensional visual sections punctuated by flashing lights. I once saw the Great Thurston who could make an elephant disappear do an act with a screen on stage. He shoots a man in the film. The actor clutches his ketchup to his tuxedo shirt and falls then Thurston steps into the screen as a detective to investigate the murder, steps back outside to commit more murders, busts in as a brash young tabloid reporter, moves out to make a phone call that will collapse the market, back in as ruined broker. I am pulled into the film in a stream of yellow light and I can pull people out of the film withdrawal shots pulling the flesh off naked boys. Sequences are linked by the presence of some arbitrary object a pin wheel, a Christmas-tree ornament, a pyramid, an Easter egg, a copper coil going away and coming in always in the same numerical order. Movement in and out of the screen can be very painful like acid in the face and electric sex tingles.

"2. Scenes that have the same enigmatic structure presented on one screen where the perspective remains constant. In a corner of the frames there are punctuation symbols. This material is being processed on a computer. I am in the presence of an unknown language spelling out the same message again and again in cryptic charades where I participate as an actor. There are also words on screen familiar words maybe we read them somewhere a long time ago written in sepia and silver letters that fade into pictures.

"3. Fragmentary glimpses linked by immediate visual impact. There is a sensation of speed as if the pictures were seen from a train window.

"4. Narrative sections in which the screens disappear. I experience a series of quite understandable and coherent events as one of the actors. The narrative sequences are preceded by the title on screen then I am in the film. The transition is painless like stepping into a dream. The structuralized peep show may intersperse the narrative and then I am back in front of the screen and moving in and out of it."

Audrey looked at the screen in front of him. His lips parted and the thoughts stopped in his mind. It was all there on screen sight sound touch at once immediate and spectrally remote in past time.

THE PENNY ARCADE PEEP SHOW

1. On screen 1 a burning red pin wheel distant amusement park. The pin wheel is going away taking the lights the voices the roller coaster the smell of peanuts and gunpowder further and further away.

2. On screens 2 and 3 a white pin wheel and a blue pin wheel going away. Audrey catches a distant glimpse of two boys in the penny arcade. One laughs and points to the other's pants sticking out straight at the crotch.

3. On screens 1 2 3 three pin wheels spinning away red white and blue. Young soldier at the rifle range beads of sweat in the down on his lip. Distant firecrackers burst on hot city pavements . . . night sky parks and ponds . . . blue sound in vacant lots.

4. On screens 1 2 3 4 four pin wheels spinning away, red, white, blue and red. A low-pressure area draws Audrey into the park. July 4, 1926 falls into a silent roller.

1. On screen 1 a red pin wheel coming in . . . smoky moon over the midway. A young red-haired sailor bites into an apple.

2. On screens 2 and 3 two pin wheels coming in white and blue light flickers an adolescent face. The pitch-

man stirs uneasily. "Take over will you kid. Gotta see a man about a monkey."

3. On screens 1 2 3 three pin wheels coming in red white and blue. A luminous post card sky opens into a vast lagoon of summer evenings. A young soldier steps from the lake from the hill from the sky.

4. On screens 1 2 3 4 four pin wheels spinning in red white blue red. The night sky is full of bursting rockets lighting parks and ponds and the upturned faces.

"The rocket's red glare the bombs bursting in air
Gave proof through the night that our flag was still there."

A light in his eyes. Must be Doctor Moor's mirror with a hole in it.

1. A flattened pyramid going away into distant bird-calls and dawn mist . . . Audrey glimpses bulbous misshapen trees . . . Indian boy standing there with a machete . . . The scene is a sketch from an explorer's notebook . . . dim in on a stained yellow page . . . "No one was ever meant to know the unspeakable evil of this place and live to tell of it . . ."

2. Two pyramids going away . . . "The last of my Indian boys left before dawn. I am down with a bad attack of fever . . . and the sores . . . I can't keep myself from scratching. I have even tried tying my hands at night when the dreams come, dreams so indescribably loathsome that I cannot bring myself to write down their content. I untie the knots in my sleep and wake up scratching . . ."

3. Three pyramids going away . . . "The sores have

eaten through my flesh to the bone and still this hideous craving to scratch. Suicide is the only way out. I can only pray that the horrible secrets I have uncovered die with me forever . . ."

4. Four pyramids going away . . . Audrey experienced a feeling of vertigo like the sudden stopping of an elevator . . . skeleton clutches a rusty revolver in one fleshless hand . . .

1. A pyramid coming in . . . Audrey can see stonework like broken lace on top of the pyramid. Damp heat closes round his body a musty odor of vegetable ferment and animal decay. Figure in a white loincloth swims out of the dawn mist. An Indian boy with rose-colored flesh and delicate features stands in front of Audrey. Two muscular Indians with long arms carry jars and tools. "You crazy or something walk around alone? This bad place. This place of flesh plants."

2. Two pyramids coming in . . . "You not careful you grow here. Look at that." He points to a limp pink tube about two feet long growing from two purple mounds covered with fine red tendrils. As the boy points to the tube it turns toward him. The boy steps forward and rubs the tube which slowly stiffens into a phallus six feet high growing from two testicles . . . "Now I make him spurt. Jissom worth much *dinero*. Jissom make flesh" . . . He strips off his loincloth and steps onto the vegetable scrotum embracing the shaft. The red hairs twist around his legs reaching up to his groin and buttocks . . .

3. Three pyramids coming in . . . The mist is lifting. In the milky dawn light Audrey sees a blush spread through the boy's body turning the skin to a swollen

red wheal. Pearly lubricant pours from the head of
the giant phallus and runs down the sides. The boy
squirms against the shaft caressing the great pulsing
head with both hands. There is a soft muffled sound,
a groan of vegetable lust straining up from tumescent
roots as the plant spurts ten feet in the air. The
bearers run around catching the gobs in stone jars.

4. Four pyramids coming in . . . The flesh garden is
located in a round crater four pyramids spaced
around it on higher ground North South East and
West. Slowly the tendrils fall away the Phallus goes
limp and the boy steps free . . . "Over there ass
tree" . . . He points to a tree of smooth red buttocks
twisted together between each buttock a quivering
rectum. Opposite the orifices phallic orchids red,
purple, orange sprout from the tree's shaft . . . "Make
him spurt too" . . . The boy turns to one of the bearers and says something in a language unknown to
Audrey. The boy grins and slips off his loincloth . . .
The other bearer followed his movements . . . "He
fuck tree. Other fuck him" . . . The two men dip
lubricant from a jar and rub it on their stiffening
phalluses. Now the first bearer steps forward and
penetrates the tree wrapping his legs around the
shaft. The second bearer pries his buttocks open with
his thumbs and squirms slowly forward men and
plant moving together in a slow hydraulic peristalsis
. . . The orchids pulse erect dripping colored drops
of lubricant . . . "We catch spurts" . . . The boy hands
Audrey a stone jar. The two boys seem to writhe into
the tree their faces swollen with blood. A choking
sound bursts from tumescent lips as the orchids spurt
like rain. "This one very dangerous" . . . The boy

points to a human body with vines growing through the flesh like veins. The body of a green pink color excretes a milky substance . . . The boy draws on parchment gloves . . . "You touch him you get sores itch you scratch spread sores feel good scratch more scratch self away" . . . Slowly the lids open on green pupils surrounded by black flower flesh. He is seeing them now you can tell. His body quivers with horrible eagerness . . . "He there long time. Need somebody pop him." . . . The boy reaches up takes the head in both hands and twists it sharply to one side. There is a sound like a stick breaking in wet towels as the spine snaps. The feet flutter and rainbow colors spiral from the eyes. The penis spurts again and again as the body twists in wrenching spasms. Finally the body hangs limp . . . "He dead now" . . . The bearers dig a hole. The boy cuts the body down and it plops into the grave . . . "Soon grow another" . . . said the boy matter of factly . . . "over there shit tree" . . . He points to a black bush in the shape of a man squatting. The bush is a maze of tentacles and caught in these tendrils Audrey sees animal skeletons . . . "Now I make him asshole" . . . The boy dipped sperm from a jar and rubbed it between the parted buttocks. Nitrous fumes rise the plant writhes in peristalsis and empties itself . . . "Very good for garden. Make flesh trees grow. Now I show you good place" . . . He leads the way up a steep path to an open place by one of the pyramids . . . In niches carved from rock Audrey sees vines growing in human forms. The figures give off a remote vegetable calm . . . "This place of vine people very calm very quiet. Live here long long time. Roots reach down to garden."

The rising sun hits Audrey in the face

⊚ Dawn light on a naked *youth* poised to dive into a pond. ———

⊚ A thousand Japanese *youths* leap from a balcony into a round swimming tank.

⊚ *Audrey* taking a shower. Water runs down his lean stomach. He is getting stiff.

⊚ Locker room toilet on five levels seen from ferris wheel . . . flash of white legs, shiny pubic hairs, lean brown arms . . . *boys* masturbating under a rusty shower.

⊚ Naked *boy* on yellow toilet seat sunlight in pubic hairs a twitching foot.

⊚ *Boys* masturbating in bleak public school toilets, outhouses, locker rooms . . . a blur of flesh.

⊚ *Farja* sighs deeply and rocks back hugging his knees against his chest. Nitrous fumes twist from pink rectal flesh in whorls of orange, sepia, rose.

⊚ Red fumes envelop the *two bodies*. A scream of roses bursts from tumescent lips roses growing through flesh tearing thorns of delight intertwined the quivering bodies crushed them together writhing gasping in an agony of roses.

⊚ What happens between my legs is like a cold drink to me it is just a feeling . . . cool round stones against my back sunshine and shadow of Mexico. It is just a feeling between the legs a sort of tingle. It is a feeling by which *I am* here at all.

⊚ We squat there our knees touching. Kiki looks down between his legs watching himself get stiff. I feel the tingle between my legs and I am getting stiff too.

- cadavers. Electron microscope shows cells, nerves, bone.
- Telescope shows stars and planets and space. Click microscope. Click telescope.

- *He* wasn't there really. Pale the picture was pale. I could see through him. In life used address I give you for that belated morning.
- Young *ghosts* blurred faces boys and workshops the old February 5, 1914.
- *I am* not a person and I am not an animal. There is something I am here for something I have to do before I can go.
- *The dead* around like birdcalls rain in my face.
- Flight of geese across a gleaming empty sky . . . Peter John S . . . 1882–1904 . . . the death of a child long ago . . . cool remote spirit to his world of shades . . . I was waiting there pale character in someone else's writing breathing old pulp magazines. Turn your face a little to eyes like forget-me-nots . . . flickering silver smile melted into air . . . The boy did not speak again.
- Cold stars splash the empty house faraway toys. Sad whispering *spirits* melt into coachmen and animals of dreams, mist from the lake, faded family photos.

- Museum bas-relief of the *God* Amen with erection. A thin boy in prep school clothes stands in the presence of the God. The boy in museum toilet takes down his pants phallic shadow on a distant wall.
- All the *Gods* of Egypt
- The *God* Amen the boy teeth bare gasping

⊙ Clear light touching marble porticos and fountains
  . . . the *Gods* of Greece . . . Mercury, Apollo, Pan

Light drains into the red walls of Marrakech

Le
Gran
Luxe

April 3, 1989 Marrakech . . . Unlighted streets carriages
with carbide lamps. It looks like an 1890 print from
some explorer's travel book. Wild boys in the streets
whole packs of them vicious as famished dogs. There is
almost no police force in operation and everyone who
can afford it has private guards. My Marrakech contact
has kindly lent me two good Nubians and found me
suitable quarters.

Waves of decoration and architecture have left a series
of strata-like exposed geologic formations. There isn't a
place in the world you can't find a piece of it in Marrakech, a St Louis street, a Mexican cantina, that house
straight from England, Alpine huts in the mountains, a
vast film set where the props are continually shifting.
The city has spread in all directions up into the Atlas

mountains to the east, south to the Sahara, westward to the coastal cities, up into the industrial reservations of the north. There are fantastic parties, vast estates and luxury such as we read about in the annals of the Roman Empire.

The chic thing is to dress in expensive tailor-made rags and all the queens are camping about in wild-boy drag. There are Bowery suits that appear to be stained with urine and vomit which on closer inspection turn out to be intricate embroideries of fine gold thread. There are *clochard* suits of the finest linen, shabby-gentility suits, Graham Greene outfits for seedy agents who are bad Catholics on a mission they don't really believe in, felt hats seasoned by old junkies, dungarees faded on farm boys, coolie clothes of yellow pongee silk, loud cheap pimp suits that turn out to be not so cheap the loudness is a subtle harmony of colors only the very best Poor Boy Shops can turn out tailored to your way of walking sitting down bending over the color of your hair and eyes your house and backdrop. It is the double take and many carry it much further to as many as six takes. Looks like an expensive suit trying rather crudely to look cheap humm the cheapness is rather carefully planned on closer inspection suits that shift changing color and texture before your eyes he is standing in what looks like a rented dress suit now the Billy Graham look no it is 120 dollar knocked down to 69.23 FBI agent suit or it could be a smooth Mexican 'pocho' beyond the Glen Plaid stage on the other hand something of an uncomfortable young cop first day in plain clothes the collar too tight the sleeves too short. All these suits were full of gimmicks, retractable sleeves, invisible pockets and not a few of the looners keep some concealed pet about their person a rat, a mongoose, a cobra, a nest of scorpions that can be suddenly released to enliven a social gathering. He appears say in a raccoon-skin coat from which leaps a live raccoon to kill Bubbles de Cocuera's six prize Chihuahuas. And Reggie in a blue mutation mongoose cape killed every cobra in the Djemalfna. Funny at first but they run it into the ground. "My God here comes Reggie in a tiger suit! Run for your lives chaps!" They will put on armor or protect themselves some way and dump almost anything into your lap. You learn to stay away from fat citizens in python suits, any swelling or protuberance is something to avoid and pregnant women have the street to themselves. Everyone has reversible linings and concealed pockets and a way to pass a pet from one pocket to the other thus foiling the searches which are now routine at the door of any gathering. The next step is skin suits and men are hunted like animals for their pelts. Then synthetics hit the market. Think of it termite-proof moth-proof age-proof in sixteen tasteful shades furniture and walls to match. People start buying anything they want a red-haired ass a Mexican crotch a Chinese stomach folks is going piebald thin black arms cracker farm boy smile then horns and goat hooves wolf boys lizard boys some frantic character got arms smooth and red as terra cotta ending in lobster claws.

There is almost no petroleum left and gasoline engines are a rarity. Steam cars and electrics are coming back. The silent electric dirigibles of the rich sail majestically across the evening sky the cabin an open-air restaurant wafting a scent of wet lawns and golf courses calm happy voices 1920 music. Le gran luxe flourishes as never before in history on the vast estates of the rich. The foremost advocate and practitioner of luxury is A.J. who owns a private steam railroad which he stocks with 1890 drummers and bankers, 1920 prep school boys on vacation, 1918 card sharps and con men according to his whim, anyone wishing to travel A.J. is required to report to casting.

"I maintain my railroads for the train whistles at lonely sidings, the smell of worn leather, steam, soot, hot iron and good cigar smoke, for the glass-covered stations and the red-brick station hotels."

He contributes lavishly to the guerrilla units, maintains a vast training center and hires fugitive scientists to develop new weapons in his laboratories and factories. He thinks nothing of spending millions of dollars to put a single dish on his table. His annual party collapses currencies and bankrupts nations.

"I want a dinner of fresh hog's liver, fried squirrel, wild asparagrass, turnip greens, hominy grits, corn on the cob and blackberries. The hog must be an Ozark razorback fed on acorns, peanuts, mulberries and Missouri apples. My hog must be kept under discreet observation round the clock to insure that it does not eat anything unclean like bullshit, baby rabbits or dead frogs the surveillance being unobtrusive so as not to render the animal self-conscious."

"When you want this by, boss? A year from now?"

"Next Sunday at the latest."

"But boss how in the hell . . . ?"

"Go to Hell if need be but find me such a hog."

"Yes boss."

"Once found he must be brought here. As you know hog's liver that has been on ice for even a few hours is quite unfit to eat. The hog must be butchered in my kitchens and the twitching liver conveyed immediately to the skillet to be cooked in the bacon grease of another such hog."

"Well sure boss . . . We could crate the hog up and jet it out here."

"Are you mad? My hog would be terrorized and this would surely have an adverse effect on its liver."

"Well boss we could take over an ocean liner fix it up like an Ozark range and . . ."

"Are you trying to poison me? The hog would become seasick and I would lose my dinner. Obviously the hog must be gently wafted here on a raft slung between two giant zeppelins, a raft lifted bodily from the Ozark Mountains. My squirrels, blackberries and wild asparagrass will of course accompany the hog and send a farm boy with it a thin boy with freckles. He will tend my hog during the trip. He will shoot and dress my squirrels. Then he will make himself useful in other ways."

"Boss the hog is here."

A.J. steps onto his balcony and there in the sky suspended between two vast blue zeppelins is a piece of Missouri trailing the smoke of hardwood forests . . .

"I want a dinner of walleyed pike, yellow perch and channel catfish from clear cold spring-fed rivers."

"Right boss I'll have a jet plane lined with aluminum and filled with water."

"Did you say *a* jet plane?"

"Sure boss."

"Mindless idiot the pike would eat the perch and the catfish would eat everything. When the plane landed there would be nothing but one gorged sluggish catfish quite unfit for my inhuman consumption. Three planes must be outfitted."

"Sorry boss but the catfish crashed. All that water slopping around and the boulders come loose."

"Praise be to Allah it was not the pike that crashed."

As a piquant offset to all this luxury there is hunger and fear and danger in the street. A man's best friends are his Colt and his Nubs experts with their staves jabbing with both ends blocking out teeth with a straight-thrust stave held level.

It is a day like any other. Breakfast in the patio served by my Malay boy. The patio is a miniature oasis with a pool, palms, a cobra, a sand fox, and some big orange lizards mean and snappy which eat melon rinds. So after breakfast I set out for the Djemalfna to meet Reggie. We are going to plan our route to A.J.'s annual party which is tomorrow it will be the do of the season. We call ourselves the "Invited" and we all have punch card invitations around our necks like dog tags that will punch us through A.J.'s electric gates. So I am cutting through the noon market sun helmet Colt cartridge belt the lot flanked by my magnificent Nubs when we run into a pack of twenty wild boys. At sight of us their eyes light up inside like a cat's will and the hair stands up straight on their heads spitting snarling they are all around us slashing at my Nubs. The leader has a patch over one eye and a hog castrator screwed into a wood and leather stump where his right hand used to be. Quick as a weasel he darts under the Nub's staff his hand flashes in and up you can feel cold steel cut intestines like spaghetti. Now it is very unchic to lose your head and use the gun for trouble the Nubs should handle like say a pack of diseased beggars. You have to decide and decide quick is this or isn't it

a Colt case. I decide it is definitely a Colt case get my
eyes converged on the leader's skinny stomach and fire.
The heavy forty-four slug knocks him ten feet. I shift and
fire shift and fire gun empty reach for my snub-nosed
thirty-eight in a special leather-lined inside breast pocket
when they scatter and fade out like ghosts. Taking inven-
tory I count seven wild boys dead or dying. The priest
darts out of a potato bin and starts giving unction. I saw
two wild boys spit at him with their last spark of life. The
Nub's eyes are glazing over, intestines steam in the noon
sun drawing flies. A policeman approaches reluctantly
and I give him some orders in crisp Arabic. I find Reggie
on the square sipping a pink gin shaded by a screen of
beggars. An old spastic woman twitches and spatters
Reggie's delicate skin with sunlight. "Uncontrolled slut!"
he screams. He turns to his henchman. "Give this worthless hag a crust of stale bread and find me a sturdy shade
beggar."

I sit down and order a Stinger. "Rumble in a square. I
lost a Nub."

"Saw it all from here. I think Donald knows about a
good Nub."

"I am burying my Nub in the American cemetery. We
can meet there and plan our route to the party. Might
have a spot of bother on the way you know."

"More than likely. A.J. has been criticized for his lavish-
ness by a few ridiculous malcontents the eternal bane
of the very rich."

Next day after the Nub is laid away with taps and all
the trimmings thirty of us join forces and set off for
A.J.'s compound which is outside the walls. Rather con-
spicuous we are too with our Nubs clad in aluminum
jockstraps and sandals carrying wire shields to screen us

from stones and at their belts for emergency use the razor-sharp machetes. So we walk along between our Nubs very *dégagé* as if we aren't actually there.

"The old man will break a stack of bricks with his karate of course it's a bore but there's no stopping him. Any case it's free meals and drinks for a month. I will say for him when he does a do it's a do."

The streets are worse than I ever see them the walking dead catatonic from hunger jammed in like so many sacks of concrete the Nubs shove with the stave the bodies bend and come right back up again they are all shuffling slowly forward and all headed for A.J.'s. From between the legs of this river of flesh the wild boys dart like vicious little cats slashing with razor blades and pieces of glass, slash and then dart back into their burrows of walking flesh. A young agent just down from West Point where they call him the Ferret he can snake through a football line like a ferret down a rat hole follows a wild boy in there and what we found after some fast machete work you don't tell the next of kin.

There it is just ahead now the electric gates thirty feet high set in a wall of black granite. Stumbling over legs we make the gate and click in while the crowd sticks its hands through the bars and shoves fingers in their mouths drooling like cows with the aftosa.

A.J. resplendent in white robes greets us from a dais over the outer courtyard. He smiles and waves to the slobbering crowd.

"They know the score right enough. The better I eat the better they eat. Le gran luxe makes tasty leavings."

The outer courtyard is a small arena with balconies around the sides. We get up in the balconies and A.J. walks down into the middle of the arena.

"Release the bull."
There is a blast of music and the bull rushes out a chute sees the old man and heads straight for him. He stands there fist drawn back and there is a light seismic tremor as he plants himself for the kill. Then his fist flashes forward and I see the brains go. The bull stumbles by him and falls on its side one leg in the air kicking spasmodically. Within seconds the carcass is butchered and the raw bleeding meat heaved to the crowd.

We go through the inner gates into the compound. There are open air restaurants serving smörgåsbord, beer, chilled aquavit and the hot fish soups of Peru, quiet riverside restaurants in blue evening shadow, red-brick houses with slate roofs whole blocks serving home-cooked American food the way they used to serve it turkey, fried chicken, iced tea, hot biscuits and corn bread, steak, roast beef, homemade strawberry ice cream, duck, wild rice, hominy grits, creamed chestnuts. There are pools and canals, floating restaurants covered with flowers, old riverboats with a menu of passenger pigeon, lark, woodcocks, wild turkey and venison, zeppelins and dining cars, chateaus of haute cuisine ruled by eccentric tyrants, Russian country sideboards with sturgeon, caviar, smoked eel, vodka, champagne and hock, farm restaurants and all varieties of plain peasant cooking, inaccessible cliff restaurants famous for a pigeon with white meat. And every famous restaurant in the world has been duplicated to the last detail, the 1001 from Tangier, the old Lucullus restaurant from Marseilles, Maxim's, the Tour D'argent, Tony Faustus from St Louis.

I notice that if anything is left on a plate or in a glass it is scraped or poured by the waiters into hampers one

for liquids the other for solids. After we have circulated
and put away what we could we are summoned to a
balcony overlooking the main gate where the poor of
Marrakech mill around waiting. A.J. harangues us
briefly on the importance of maintaining a strong be-
nevolent image in the native mind and at this point a
panel slides back in the wall on one side of the gate
and a huge phallus slides out pissing Martinis, soup,
wine, Coca-Cola, grenadine, vodka, bourbon, beer, hot
buttered rum, pink gin, Alexanders, glog, corn whisky
into a trough forty feet long labeled DRINKS. From a
panel on the other side of the gate a rubber asshole
protrudes spurting out Baked Alaska, salted herring,
duck gravy, chili con carne, peach melba, syrups,
sauces, jam, fat bone and gristle into another trough
labeled EATS. Screaming clawing drooling the crowd
throws itself at the troughs scooping up food and drinks
with both hands. The odor of vomit rises in clouds. A.J.
presses a button that seals the balcony over. Ventilators
whir and a smell of cool summer pools and mossy
stones envelops the guests. We all stay a month which
isn't hard to do considering what is inside and what is
outside.

In addition to the restaurants of the compound culinary
expeditions on location to all parts of the globe are or-
ganized for the more vigorous guests. The guests are up
at six for a breakfast of fruit juice, fried eggs perfectly
cooked so that the yolk runs slowly when you cut it,
bacon that bends slightly over the fork neither too
crisp nor too limp, homemade bread, tea and coffee a
cigarette and a rest and they start out through the flaming autumn hills. It is a bright blue October day. They
walk ten miles to a river where the flatboats are waiting.

The river is cold and clear and deep. They float down-stream fishing along the way in pools and bays and in-lets. Tying up the boats for lunch the guests arm themselves with springy clubs and walk along the bank killing frogs and skinning the legs which they fry in bacon grease and eat crisp with cold beer. By late after-noon when they arrive at the farm ferry they have an ample string of jack salmon (also known as walleyed pike), black bass, perch and channel cat. Red-brick house on the hill bourbon and marijuana grown in Mis-souri summer heat on poor hill soil has a special tang, purple weed they call it. A twilight like blue dust sifting into the river valley as they sit down to a meal of jack salmon steaks, fried perch and bass cooked in bacon grease with a faint smoky tang cider and apples from the farm orchard. They hunt through the autumn woods and return to a dinner of quail, wild turkey and squirrel with chestnuts, spring onions and sweet potatoes. Other locations feature skiing in preparation for smörgåsbord with chilled aquavit, hot chili dishes after a ride through the mountains of northern Mexico, lobsters and clams on the beach, iced tea and fried chicken at The Green Inn.

Food is only one attraction. Every pleasure, sport, di-version, interest, hobby, pursuit or instruction is pro-vided for. To list some of the facilities: computerized libraries with complete references on any subject, ex-pert instructors on any subject, sport or skill. There are gliders, balloons, parachutes, aqualungs and deep-sea diving from the coastal estates. There are sense-with-drawal chambers, immersion tanks, no-gravity capsules simulating space conditions. There are ranges where you can practice with every weapon from a laser gun to a boomerang. There are blue movies of incomparable artistry. Every period of history and every place or country is represented in A.J.'s International Pavilion. You can enjoy a trip to the 1920's, Renaissance Italy, Mandarin China, ancient Greece or Rome. Every sexual taste is provided for in any setting you want. Jack off in the 1920's? Fuck temple virgin? You make Gemini with nice astronaut? Greek youths clad only in beauty and sunlight? Forecastle on whaling ship? Afternoon in the Roman baths? See me fuck Cleopatra? Kinky Chimu kicks? Sex in a 1910 outhouse? Rumble seat? Bomb shelter in the blitz? Bedroll for two in the Yukon? The old swimming hole? Viking ship? Bedouin tent? Public school toilet? Anything that you like.

This morning after a breakfast of fruit, yogurt and pheasant eggs I walk over to the glider hangar. A.J. has several hundred gliders derived from the early models you launch by running and land on your feet sometimes. There are gliders that can be launched from skis, roller skates and bicycles. In all cases the gliders have been designed to most closely approximate the dream of wings and flight. If you have your own ideas for a new model the designers will make it up for you in a few days. The gliders are of many materials and colors to match different landscapes and sky conditions and many of them are painted with landscapes. There are red models for sunset gliding, transparent plastic for ski gliding, blue wings for the mountains. I select a mountain model that shades from lightest egg blue to blue black. The wings are of ramie fabric. A small electric dirigible takes us to the launching station up in the

Atlas mountains. From the station a steep concrete runway slopes down. I put on roller skates and pick up the glider, the wings on each side my hands braced on two struts. The ship is piloted by shifting weight with the hands the pilot being suspended between two struts at the center. When your arms get tired there is a sling seat. I start down the launching run faster faster knees bent I zoom right off across the valley legs dangling over two thousand feet of space. This is really flying like you do in a dream, piloting the glider with both hands feeling it vibrate through me I am out there now in the wings, my wings sailing across the valley. I sit down on the sling seat and see the city spread out between my legs. I bring it down on a cracked weed-grown subdivision street and skate back to the compound for an afternoon in the blue movies.

Some years ago the actors went on strike protesting conditions prejudicial to their dignity.

"Your flesh diseased dirty pictures how long you want us to fuck very nice Meester Slastobitch? We is fucking tired of fuck very nice." Accordingly the great Slastobitch introduced a series of reforms. Considering the demands of the workers he decided that the blue movies must have story, character development and background in which sex scenes are incidental. For example a story of a whaling voyage 1859 two hours in length contains only eighteen minutes of sex scenes scattered through the film.

"The blue movies as a separate genre have ceased to exist. We show sex as it occurs in the story as a part of life not a mutilated fragment."

I go to the old Palace Theatre on Market Street. The

first number is an educational short showing how le gran luxe can be achieved on a modest income.

"Now here is my immersion trough in the blue room just a trough full of glycerine sheet aluminum I got it all through the PX for almost nothing my dear now if you'll just slip into this plastic cover Yage and Majoun for this trip Majoun is good on a bluie your first solo my dear and you are well prepared you see it's all so simple home is where your ass is and if you want to move you move your ass the first step is learning to change homes with someone else and have someone else's ass. I remember a science-fiction thing about an institute called Fishook given over to paranormal psychic things they have a box they get in and their minds travel to other planets. Well one of these planets is so 'evil' it drives an astronaut back to the Bible Belt where he preaches up a holy war against the 'Parries' they are called and by now everyone outside Fishook hates the 'Parries' and there are signs up 'Parry, Don't Let The Sun Set On You Here.' And Fishook has closed the doors whole villages of nice old 'Parries' and the teen-age 'Parries' all bucking for Fishook will be slaughtered."

But there is another astronaut on the lam from Fishook security who knows about a nice quiet planet and he wants to rescue all good "Parries" everywhere but how to transport the paranormal assholes? In a flash the know-how comes to him from that "evil" planet and when he tells the villagers what to do they say
"But that's dirty."
"Not dirty just alien" he says. "Besides you don't have much choice." He points to a long row of headlights approaching the paranormal village. "The vigilantes

are on the way. So you see it's time to move on. And what you find outside is only what you put there in the first place. Time to move into first place."

He was lying on a bed in his shorts split bamboo walls top floor of the hotel. A knock at the door. The Indian boy stood there a quart beer bottle in one hand. "*Aquí Yage Ayahuasca . . . muy bueno . . . muy fuerte . . .*" The boy came in closing the door and put the bottle on a table. The American boy who was thin and blond got two tin cups from his rucksack. The Indian boy poured out the mixture from the beer bottle filling each cup two-thirds full. He passed his hands back and forth over the cups humming a little tune. He stopped humming looked at the American and smiled.

"This very good for fuck Johnny." He made a tight brown fist and shoved a finger in and out. "We take Yage then fuck." He unbuttoned his shirt. "*Ambos nudo Johnny* . . . both naked." He dropped his shirt on a chair, kicked off his sandals, shoved his pants and shorts down. He waited until the American was stripped. "Now take Yage . . . act very fast." The American drank and shuddered. "*Muy amargo sí Johnny.*"

Almost at once the American boy felt a blue tide cool evening air on his naked rectum his legs . . . "*Tomamos eso . . . ambos nudo*" . . . shadows fading hand on a tin cup eyes smiling and knowing the bare rectum the other was looking pressure the groin facing each other . . . "*Vuelvete*" . . . getting hard in the blue light . . . "Bend over Johnny" . . . The boy picked up a tin of Vaseline and slowly with a calm intent expression rubbed it on his cock . . . "Bend over Johnny and spread ass" . . . feeling the eyes and fingers on his rectum ass hairs spread the slow penetration . . . "Hand on knees Johnny" . . . He twisted his body in a slow circle hands braced on knees stirring whirlpools of blue tighter tighter tighter spurting blue Chinese characters in the purple dusk of Lima gasps "*muy bueno*" hands on knees Carl's eyes sputtering blue his face blurred out bone-wrenching spasms popped egg-blue worlds in air a wake of jissom across the sky.

"Now I've been thinking of a communal immersion tank in the swimming pool but I may make a fish pond instead. Really it should be filled with raw oysters and . . ." A trough cut in pink coral dome-shaped room lined with sea shells the boy spread his legs and squirms down into the oysters the tight conch of his nuts spurting pearly gobs sea wind through a porthole. "Yes of course they are soundproof rooms in various degrees but we do have sound tracks and odors now in the blue room ozone and burning leaves and in the red room roses and carbolic soap Lifebuoy isn't making it any more but you can still get it down here and I've laid in several cases now here is the rainbow room for Dim-N and Psylocybin rather tacky isn't it smell of orange crush plastics and carnivals you come the world's fair my dear and of course I need a yellow room but there are so few Chinese boys in Casa I haven't gotten to it but you can see the daffodils and crocuses whiffs of straw and urine and saffron and ambergris the yellow tower of amber chamois pallet the boy yellow hair brown eyes teeth bared coming inside out and of course you mix your skin colors say black and red brown and yellow red and white rather limited here but we don't do too badly and the sound tracks distant train whistles and fog horns for the blue room sea sounds in the pink room and music special for the two parties and sometimes more than two of course. Is your Majoun working? I need a laboratory to work out all the drug prob-

lems synthesis, blending new formulae now if you are
taking Majoun which works so much slower than Yage
or Dim-N you have to wait two hours on the Majoun.
Oh! here's Ali . . . Now if you'll put on these head-
phones Genua music in the blue room of course you'll
find the Yage already measured out."

When the music started in his head the lower half of
his body came loose in fluid gyrations come yell cracked
his head rainbow room stars on the table knees of
amber brown teeth bared.

"And the image track of course we take movies and mix
the movies all up with color shots blue mist and attic
rooms under slate roofs sunsets autumn leaves apples
red moon in the smoky sky all mixed with sex pictures
we take five or six cameras one on the face one on the
genitals twitching feet coming eyes and usually we pro-
ject these in the white room which has plain white walls
for screens a rainbow cocktail of LSD Majoun Yage
very little LSD it isn't good for you really and the natural plants are better."

Red-haired boy on his side chewing his knuckles as the
Arab boy browns him pictures on the walls and ceilings
five projectors a kaleidoscope of legs, spurting cocks,
tight nuts, eyes, faces, a twitching foot, sunsets and
blue mist, urine in straw, yellow sky, quivering buttocks, sperm spurting vapor trails, snow-capped mountains, rainbows, Niagara Falls, souvenir post cards,
Northern lights as the boy turns him with his knees up
he is on top looking at the ceiling pictures now on
hands and knees both facing the wall come seeing themselves in television mixed in with all the others "right
on location but rather over our budget I'm afraid so
lucky to find all these dome-shaped rooms rather like

the inside of a huge phallus aren't they now here is the
rose room."

Red bed cover sprinkled with rose petals feeling the red
egg in his groin spurting sunsets, freckles, red hair,
autumn leaves, knees up he was coming in the autumn
sky.

The Penny Arcade Peep Show

1. A round red Christmas tree ornament going away
. . . Indian boy with bright red gums spits blood
under the purple dusk of Lima.
"Fight tuberculosis folks."
Christmas Eve . . . An old junky selling Christmas
seals on North Clark Street. The "Priest" they called
him.
"Fight tuberculosis folks."

2. Two round ornaments going away one blue one
green . . . fading train whistles blue arc lights flickering empty streets half buried in sand . . . jelly in green
brown rectal flesh twisting finger turns to vine tendril
ass hairs spread over the tide flats . . . sea weed . . .
green pullman curtains . . . blue prep school clothes.

3. Three ornaments going away red, blue, green . . . Holly wreaths, red ribbons, children bobbing for apples . . . It was getting late and no money to score he turned into a side street and the lake wind hit him like a knife . . . a lost street of brick chimneys and slate roofs . . . heavy blue silence . . . lawn sprinklers summer golf course . . . *The Green Hat* folded on her knee.

4. Four ornaments going away red, blue, green, gold . . . freckles, autumn leaves, smoky red moon over the river
"When the autumn weather turns the leaves to flame
And I haven't got time for a waiting game."

Cab stopped just ahead under a street light and a boy got out with a suitcase thin kid in blue prep school clothes familiar face the "Priest" told himself watching from a doorway reminds me of something a long time ago the boy there with his overcoat unbuttoned reaching into his pants pockets for the cab fare . . . blue magic of all movies in remembered kid standing at the attic window waving to a train . . . a sighing sound the empty room . . . distant smell of weeds in vacant lots little green snakes under rusty iron . . . pirate chests pieces of eight on golden sands . . . urine in straw . . . the Traveller walks on and on through the plain of yellow grass. He stops by a deep black pool. A yellow fish side turns in the dark water.

1. Red ornament coming in . . . red leg hairs rubbing rose wall paper . . . Irish terrier under the Christmas tree . . . light years away the pale skies fall apart. T.B. waiting at the next stop. Spit blood at dawn. I was waiting there.
"Doctor Harrison. They called me."

Led the way up . . . stairs worn red carpeting . . . smell of sickness is in the room.

2. Two ornaments coming in one blue one green . . . blue evening shadows a cool remote Sunday . . . dead stars drifting . . . twisting coming in green brown rectal flesh grass stains on brown knees.

3. Three ornaments coming in red, blue, green . . . smell of roses, carbolic soap . . . there was nothing for me to do. Spit blood at dawn. Agony to remember the words . . . "Too late" . . . German living room outside the China blue northern sky and drifting clouds . . . bad seascapes of the dying medical student.
"A schnapps I think Frau Underschnitt."
Room over the florist shop flower smell green curtains . . . He was a caddy it seems. His smile across the golf course.

4. Four ornaments coming in red, blue, green, gold . . . heart pulses in the rising sun . . . smell of raw meat . . . the heretic spits boiling blood . . . 18th Century room . . . snow at the latticed window . . . fire in the hearth . . . An old gentleman wrapped in red shawls is measuring laudanum into a medicine glass . . . Have you seen Patapon Rose? . . . blue shadows in the attic room . . . the boy's picture is framed in forget-me-nots . . . dust on the broken greenhouse . . . in the ruined garden a pool is covered with green slime . . . thin blond boy . . . sunlight in pubic hairs . . . I remember daffodils and yellow wallpaper . . . a gold watch that played "Silver Threads Among the Gold" . . . an old book with gilt edges . . . in golden letters . . . The Street of Chance.

Dim far away the Star of Bethlehem from the school play.

The Miracle of the Rose

June 23, 1988. Today we got safely through the barrier and entered the Blue Desert of Silence. The silence is devastating at first you drown in it our voices are muted as if we were speaking through felt. I have two guides with me Ali a Berber lad with bright blue eyes and yellow hair a wolfish Pan face unreadable as the sky. The other Farja of a dusky rose complexion with long lashes straight black hair gums a bright red color. We are wearing standard costumes for the area: blue silk knee-length shorts, blue silk shirts, Mercury sandals and helmets. The Mercury sandals and helmets once fitted are never removed. We are carrying nothing but light mattresses, mess kits, rations of dried fish, rice, peppers, dates, brown sugar and tea. It is a beautiful country and the predominant color is blue. Like many so-called deserts it is far from being a desert. There are wooded areas and we glimpse bodies of water from time to time. In the late afternoon we came to a vast deserted city streets cracked and broken weeds growing through houses and villas all empty overgrown with vines the scent of flowers always heavier in the air like a funeral parlor and no sign of life in the ruined courtyards empty hotels and cafés. As the sun was setting we took a road leading out of the city. None of us wanted to camp for the night in that necropolis of silent flowers. On a hill over the city we came to a ruined villa covered with rose vines. The building was in ruins little more than the walls remaining and it was not a place I would have chosen to camp. But Ali stopped and pointed. He said something in a low voice to Farja who looked down sulkily and bit his lip. Ali took a flute from his belt. Playing a little piper tune he stepped forward and we followed. Exploring the ruin we found a room with rose wallpaper. Two walls remained the support posts and bare beams of the ceiling covered with rose vines formed an arbor. Rose petals had fallen on the faded pink coverlet of a brass bed. As soon as we found this room Ali seemed possessed by a curious excitement. He prowled about like a cat playing his flute. He turned to Farja and said one word I did not catch. Farja stood there his eyes downcast blushing and trembling. He looked at the bed the walls and the rose vines. He nodded silently and the blood rushed to his face. The two boys stripped to their sandals and helmets. Farja's whole body was blushing to his sandals. His skin is a dusky rose color the genitals perfectly formed neither small nor large black shiny pubic hairs precise as wires. He poised and cleared the bed stand in a leap that carried him to the center of the bed on hands and knees. Then he rolled over and lay on his back with the knees up. Ali stood at the foot of the bed. Like all so-called the boy lay down with his knees up gasping late afternoons deserted streets slow pressure of semen rectal smell of flowers two naked bodies bathed in smoky rose of the dying sun phantom bed from an old movie set long since abandoned to weeds and vines. Their eyes locked and they breathed together. I could see Farja's heart pulsing under the dusky flesh and Ali's heart beating with his. Both phalluses stiffened to the blood drums and throbbed erect. On the tip of each phallus a pearl of lubricant squeezed out. Farja sighed deeply and rocked back holding his knees. Nitrous fumes twisted from the pink rectal flesh in whorls of orange and sepia. A musty odor filled the air that sent blood pounding and singing in my ears. The sepia fumes cleared and Farja's rectum was a quivering breathing rose of flesh. With a quick movement Ali stepped over the bed stand and kneeled in front of the rose breathing deeply his lips swollen with blood. The rose pulled his loins forward and breathed his phallus in. Red fumes enveloped the two bodies. A scream of roses burst from tumescent lips roses growing in flesh tearing thorns of delight intertwined their quivering bodies crushed them together writhing gasping choking in an agony of roses sharp reek of sperm.

Sepia picture in an old book with gilt edges. THE MIRACLE OF THE ROSE written in gold letters. I turn the page. A red color that hurts transparent roses growing through flesh the other leans forward drinking roses from his mouth their hearts translucent roses squirming in naked agony blushing gasping the air of empty hotels mouth speaking of a brass bed luminous excitement on his back with the knees up red fumes that burn erogenous holes in writhing flesh naked choking in that phantom bed when I came to the room was abandoned to weeds and vines star dust on a bench silent empty room kid of darkness fading over the florist shop flickering look an old wash stand musty house slow smile you there dim jerky bedroom 18 on the top floor : : : my flesh : : : I could : : : the film breaks : : : jerky silent film : : : look at the fading body : : : I looked about nineteen. "But not that one word?" It is getting dark : : : boy : : : remember so intense it hurts : : : sadness in his eyes 1920 movie : : : peanuts : : : "Thank you" : : : the film breaks : : : naked boy on yellow toilet fingers from a long time ago the boy solid quick and silent coming so intense it hurts teeth bared see solid now I could touch my flesh pants down evening sky : : : naked boy fading erased out : : : "Thank you" : : : the film breaks : : : pose is a long time ago memory noises frayed magazine over there room grainy like an old movie dim silver sky : : : the other leans forward laughing comparing : : : pieces of the blurred 1920 afternoon : : : jerky bed twisted feet buttocks quivering phantom boy nods the other straddles rectum exposed squeezed out musty odor luminous bodies quiver together deserted city dying sun old movie set. I turn the page. Sepia of each phallus a drop of the red color that hurts blood pounding singing naked rectum breathing rose flesh mouth speaking prickles of delight. I turn the page each picture framed in roses.

The Proposition. a ruined wall with rose paper the bed. Ali points to the bed. Farja stands there sullen eyes downcast long lashes.

The Agreement. Farja looks at the bed blushing to his bare feet.

The Consummation. Roses and thorns through translucent flesh squirming a slow scream of roses. I turn the page.

The Elixir of the Rose. Farja knees up rectum rose pulsing. The monk drains off a red fluid that flows from his translucent phallus.

The Tree of Flesh. A musty odor rises from the pages. A Mayan priest is drawing the flesh sap from a bulbous phallic tree. He has inserted an obsidian tube into the soft flesh of the tree and is draining the sap into a stone jar.

Discovery of the Jars. A Mayan pyramid. The monks have broken a door and found the jars.

The Flesh Sheets. The monk has rolled sheets of the flesh sap out on a table. The flesh sap is of a pearly grey color.

The Writing. The monk is writing on the sheets the pictures from an old book.

The Body Builder. The monk is wrapping flesh sheets around the two skeletons. Two youths have been formed. Mouth rectum and penis sealed.

The Creation. The monk has arranged the youth on a canopy knees up. He picks up a crystal phallic jar of the elixir. He lets a drop fall between the parted buttocks a drop on the end of the penis. With a crystal rod he rubs a drop on the lips. Where the fluid touches nitrous fumes arise sepia orange dusky rose. The lips part rectum quivers phallus spurts. The youth is breathing. I turn the page.

The Academy. red-brick building over a river autumn leaves the rising sun.

Morning Sleep. Naked boy with a hard-on sleeping lips parted. Roommate stands at the foot of the bed with sheet he has just pulled off the other.

The Awakening. The boy's eyes looking down at his erection blushing to his bare feet as he sees other standing there.

The Recognition. The other has dropped the sheet from his naked body laughing comparing sepia gobs in air.

The Proposition. Two boys in the room. "That's kid stuff. I wanta." One boy with eyes downcast sullen.

The Agreement. Rose of flesh on all fours quivering in a red haze. He pulls Jerry over on top of him Jerry knees up feet in the air kicking like a frog. John reaches down rubs lubricant around the tip of Jerry's cock pumping his slow deep ecstasy as they squirm together knees up kicking out the spurts. Ali plays the flute. Two boys by a pool on all fours faces turned to the full moon light June knees. Ali points to the silent YES.

At dawn the two boys got up and walked out naked into the ruined garden. Coming to a thick tangle of rosebushes Farja leaped through and emerged untouched by the thorns on the other side and then I jumped a sweet tearing pain landed on hands and knees fell forward on my elbows gasping feeling the rose in my trembling buttocks a red steam along the backs of my thighs as Farja kneeled behind me. Ali sat on the edge of a pool playing his flute dangling his feet in the black water. The boy stands holding a sheet in front of his body turned to the full moon. He drops the sheet. Boys laughing comparing sepia pictures. I turn the page. The Proposi-

tion. Ali points to the rectum. Frayed magazine one
with eyes down on the pages and pictures quivering
mouth turned to the full moon boy just pulled off the
other getting browned there coming gobs in the air
sulky youth a silent YES blushing buttocks. Ali points
to the rectum. Downcast eyes to his bare feet blushing
erogenous roses the agony of that color so intense it
hurts quivering prickles of delight deserted city rose
vines empty hotels boys laughing comparing sepia
knees. "Kid stuff. I wanta." The Agreement on all fours
parted buttocks bare feet in an old book dusk by a pool
the youth breathing deeply sullen eyes downcast and
the slow YES sweet pain blushing red steam along his
thighs spasms of delight thorns through the buttocks.
I turn the page feeling the rose twist alive in my flesh.
Dawn eyes tight knees the youth breathing from his
mouth the slow YES erogenous agony the body writes
out musty odors squeezed to the full moon. A sighing
sound back. The film breaks. An old book with gilt
stars silver paper fingers from another memory naked
shorts and shirt there a fourteen-year-old boy flesh
steaming.

Look at that compass of age and wind. Mister about?
Dim jerky bed is there. I am the empty room pieces
of the dim picture a rustle of darkness fading. Now
I remember so intense it hurts. Mrs Murphy's rooming house. They got up remembered "Thank you."
Room eighteen on the top floor background grainy
like an old movie. The film breaks. Kid standing there
talking to another. There are two. They got up naked
shorts and shirts there room eighteen on the top floor
my flesh steaming.

We tried various ways of slipping the tight blue shorts

down over the Mercury sandals but any way you slip
the feathers are being rubbed the wrong way. It is not
hot. It is not cold. There are no noxious animals or in-
sects. A fresh wind sprang up and wafted my blue
shorts away. So we wave good-by to shirt and shorts.
Ali is fucking Farja on all fours. His wolfish eyes light
up inside and the hair stands up on his head. Then
they did a hot Mercury crackling all over with blue fire
and a classic Mercury with porticos and glades and
pools. We lie there on the magic carpet of shared bodies
the old fear of the border cities still heard still felt.
Farja shudders in his sleep.

We are in an area of electric sex currents. Suddenly we
get prickles in the crotch and then pictures start of
what we are going to do like you are watching a picture
of yourself doing it and you plop right into the screen
with a delicious squeeze, Ali and Farja chasing and
wrestling each other in and out of the film. We camped
in a ruined signal tower on a promontory of land jutting
out over the desert. We reached it at twilight a blue
mist settling on the narrow flagstone path, a rusty gate
a sign overgrown with vines: U.S. Army Reservation.
Authorized Personnel Only. The old M.P. box still there.
The boys give it a push and it crashes into the valley.
Here is the old tower. We climb up to the control room
great laser guns broken the top of the tower blasted
away. We camp there and after the evening meal Ali
brings out his flute and we follow the music further and
further out into the silence.

The following day we find ourselves walking down a
country road red clay pieces of flint here and there.
Farja finds an arrowhead. We came to a deserted village of red-brick houses with slate roofs by a stream.

1. An Easter egg with a peephole going away . . . bits of vivid and vanishing detail . . . rainbow a post card road . . . boy there by the creek bare feet twisted on a fence.

2. Two Easter eggs going away . . . ghostly flower smell by the stagnant creek the boy still there waiting.

3. Three Easter eggs going away . . . click of distant heels . . . footsteps on a windy street . . . sad open hand.

4. Four Easter eggs going away . . . empty streets half-buried in sand . . . a house . . . a weed-grown golf course . . . blue prep school clothes further and further away.

1. An egg coming in . . . Road corner stone bridge rainbow over a stream green fields . . . Boy there naked. He is lying on his stomach eating an apple legs curled over his thighs. He claps his feet together. A book is open in front of him on the grass.

2. Two eggs coming in . . . sad old human papers I carry . . . two adolescents by the garage faraway toy cars.

3. Three eggs coming in . . . Smell of carbolic soap . . . Three boys in shower. A boy turns mocking him off.

4. Four eggs coming in. Audrey squeezes through the peephole wet dream tension tingling in his crotch. He is in the shower with John on a Saturday afternoon. They are facing each other Audrey uneasy feeling John's eyes on his body . . . "Wanta feel something nice Audrey?" . . . John reaches forward with soapy fingers feeling Audrey's crotch . . . sudden raw hard-on.

Dim dead boy so I haunted your old flower smell of young nights on musty curtains empty prep school clothes further and further away. Come closer. Listen across empty back yards and ash pits.

He is bending over in the shower while John washes his back glancing down along his stomach to the crotch biting his lip hoping that John will finish before he gets out of control. John is rubbing soap just above the buttocks. He leans forward and says in Audrey's ear . . . "Wanta feel something nice Audrey?" . . . John slides a finger up his ass and jiggles it to a car horn outside. Audrey drops his head gasping as his body contracts squeezing out the hot spurts.

American house . . . rain outside . . . boy standing by the ghost car . . . sunset . . . blue clothes . . . the phone rings . . . child voice across a distant sky . . . "Long long expected call from you" . . . fingers from the phone like wood. Audrey drying himself carefully trying to keep it down. He turned away holding a towel in front of him. John reached out and pulled the towel away looking at Audrey's half-erection . . . "You ever been goosed Audrey?" . . . Audrey shook his head blushing . . . "Lean over and brace your hands on your knees" . . . He heard John unscrew a jar then felt the greased finger slide up him. He gasped and threw his head back . . . "You ever been rosed Audrey?" . . . Thumbs prying his buttocks apart as John squirmed forward. Pink eggs popped in his crotch.

Souvenir post cards a violet evening sky rising from the boy's groin . . . sad 1920 scraps . . . dim jerky far-away stars splash the stagnant creek . . . "I was waiting there" . . . held a little-boy photo in his withered hand . . . The boy was footsteps down the windy street a long time ago.

Silver light popped in his eyes.

A
Silver
Smile

Tonight Reggie and I had dinner with the Great Slastobitch and he expounded the new look in blue movies.
"The movies must first be written if we are to have
living characters. A writer may find it difficult to make
the reader see a scene clearly and it would seem easier
to show pictures. No. The scene must be written before
it is filmed.

"The new look in blue movies stresses story and character. This is the space age and sex movies must express
the longing to escape from flesh through sex. The way
out is the way through." He switches on a projector.
"The scene where Johnny has crabs and Mark makes
him undress . . .

"Who are these boys? Where will they go? They will become astronauts playing the part of American married

idiots until the moment when they take off on a Gemini expedition bound for Mars, disconnect and leave the earth behind forever" . . . (It happened a few minutes after take-off. The screen went dead. The radio went dead. The astronauts had disconnected. There was a talk of space madness.)

Mark's wife told reporters: "He frightened me at times. There was something in him I could never quite reach." John's wife said: "He was a dutiful husband but I never got any warmth out of him." (The FBI did not publicize the fact that they had found in a locked drawer of John's desk a number of muscle magazines.)

The sex scenes of their adolescence are seen as image dust in space through which they pass to other planets. The set is the 1920's. Sex scenes are intercut with lawn sprinklers, country clubs, summer golf courses, classrooms, silver stars, morning sleep of detour, frogs in 1920 roads, cocktail shakers, black Cadillacs, cool basement toilets, a boy's twitching foot, the Charleston, iced tea and fried chicken at The Green Inn, 1920 ponds, naked boy hugging his knees sunlight in pubic hairs.

A suburban room afternoon light bleakly clear. Mark is eighteen. He is stripped to his shorts reading a copy of *Amazing Stories* one leg thrown over the arm of a chair. He is smoking a cigarette. The other boy John is fifteen, thin, pale, his face spattered with adolescent pimples. He is barefoot dressed in khaki pants and a white shirt. Without looking up from his magazine Mark says: "I heard you got laid the other night."

"Oh! uh! yes . . . down on Westminster Place."

"Like it?"

"Well uh! I guess it was all right," says the boy dubiously.

"Maybe it isn't what you want."

The boy John is standing by the window looking out. He scratches his crotch.

"I itch something awful."

Lazily Mark drops his magazine on the floor. He looks at Johnny through cigarette smoke. "You itch Johnny? Where?"

John turns from the window. "Right here" he says scratching his crotch.

"Come over here Johnny."

Johnny walks over in front of the chair. Mark spreads his legs. Right here." Johnny stands in front of him between his knees.

"Drop your pants Johnny."

"Huh? Why?"

"Just drop your pants like I tell you. I wanta see something."

Johnny fumbles awkwardly with his belt.

"I'll do it." Mark unbuckles Johnny's belt. With gentle precise fingers he unbuttons pants and shorts and shoves them down. They fall to Johnny's ankles. Johnny stands there his cock half-up from the scratching mouth dry heart pounding. Mark reaches forward and takes Johnny's cock by the tip with two fingers moving it to one side and with the other hand parts pubic hairs. He points to red mark . . . "Look there Johnny" . . . Oh! Christ! it is happening he can't stop it. Mark looks up at him and Johnny blushes bright red biting his lip. Mark smiles slow and brings his finger up in three jerks as Johnny's cock stands out all the way up and throbs to his pounding heart.

Sunlight in pubic hairs sad muscle magazines over the florist shop pants down green snakes under rusty iron

in the vacant lot the old family soap opera lock of
yellow hair stirs in September wind shirt open on the
golf course grass squeezed under quivering hard-ons
wet grass between his legs pale buttocks sex sweat dim
jerky faraway toilet pants down looking down now
twisted slow smile . . . "Relax Johnny. It happens" . . .
The old film stops . . . naked boy on yellow toilet seat
buttocks quivering smell of rectal mucous windy
oranges I remember a dim building overgrown with
disuse and later in Mexico City I see myself looking at
him as if trying to focus to remember who the stranger
was standing under a dusty tree lean and ragged ruffled
brown hair blue eyes vacant blank I remember London
stairs worn red carpeting and I could see his pants were
sticking up between his legs colored photo had something written on it . . . *"Vuelvete y aganchete"* . . . I let
myself go limp inside blank factual he slid it in out
through the little dusty window afternoon hills the old
broken point of origin St Louis Missouri emaciated
body head on the grimy pillow my face . . . The film
stops in his eyes . . . blue morning naked boy on yellow
toilet seat a quivering foot in front of the wash stand
soapy hands turned to me and finished machine gun
noises as he came street shadows his distant hand there
it is just to my shoulder smell of sickness in the room a
shooting star silence floats down on falling leaves and
blood spit the smell of decay shredded to dust and
memories pieces of legs and cocks and assholes drifting
fragments in sunlight ass hairs spread on the bed dust
of young hand fading flickering thighs and buttocks
smell of young nights.

One day we come home very tired and fall asleep naked
in the bed. We wake up and the room is full of moon

light. Kiki is lying there on his face and says he is very
stiff and sore from carrying clubs all day will I rub his
back. I start at the shoulder and work down to his ass
and run my hands along the back of his thighs and he says
. . . *"Más Johnny . . . Más"* . . . So I shove his ass apart
with both hands and jiggle it and he keeps saying . . .
"Más . . . Más" . . . I dip my finger in Vaseline not let-
ting him see what I am doing and rub my finger around
his ass outside at first and he says . . . *"Más . . . Más"*
. . . So I twist my finger around until it sinks all the
way in up to his pearl and he sighs and says . . . *"Más
. . . Más"* . . . And I say . . . *"Qué más Kiki?"* . . . He
doesn't want to say it but I keep twisting my finger and
he is squirming and finally he says . . . "Fucking me
Johnny" . . . *"Apartate las piernas"* . . . .He spreads his
legs and I slide it in slow feeling the ring squeeze me
and I can tell when he spurts. Afterward he doesn't
want to turn over and show me but I turn him over and
his juice is silver in the moonlight.

Next day he says it didn't happen and slaps me when I
try to do it but a few nights later he gets out of bed
to put out a cigarette leaning forward on the table and
I stand up behind him spit on my finger and slide it up
his ass all the way and he just sighs and falls forward
with his elbows on the table and looks at me over his
shoulder and says . . . *"Qué me haces Johnny?"* . . . I
get the Vaseline and rub it in standing behind him
hitch my arms around his hips and shove it in we are
standing in front of the mirror I can see my white rump
pumping and he had his head down on his hands biting
his knuckles and whimpering. I reach around and play
with his eggs and pull his foreskin back gently he gasps
and I am feeling the scratchy pressure all the way up
pumping him inside we are both coming. I can feel

goose pimples on my back and then suddenly an electric
shiver and my hair stands up straight and I can see my
eyes light up inside like a cat.

Johnny stands in front of Mark tight pants slow finger
reaches up and unbuttons his fly parting pubic hairs
points to a red mark . . . "You got crabs Johnny. Come
in the bathroom" . . . Mark locks the door . . . "All right
Johnny. Strip down" . . . Awkwardly Johnny takes off
his shirt and hangs it on the bathroom door. Mark
spreads a yellow towel on the toilet seat . . . "Take off
your pants and shorts and sit there" . . . Johnny swal-
lows feeling cold in the stomach . . . "All right" . . .
Mouth dry heart pounding he sits down naked on the
toilet seat. Mark selects a bottle of Campho-Phenique
from the medicine cabinet. He squats in front of
Johnny. Their knees touch . . . "Spread your legs apart
so I can see what I'm doing" . . . He opens the bottle
and tips it against his finger. He lifts Johnny's penis by
the tip moving it around as he rubs the camphorated oil
in pubic hairs at the root. The oil leaves a cold burn.
Johnny licks his lips and blushes . . . "Christ Mark" . . .
Mark rests his hands on Johnny's and looks up at
Johnny who blushes to his bare feet as his cock floats
up throbbing . . . "Relax Johnny. It happens" . . . He
rubs the oil around Johnny's tight nuts. Johnny's embarrassment changes to excitement. He squirms and a drop
of lubricant squeezes slowly out the end of his phallus
and glitters in the afternoon sun . . . "You take off *your*
shorts" . . . "Sure Johnny" . . . Mark squirms his shorts
off . . . "Like I say it happens" . . . The two boys look
at each other. "You probably got them in your ass too.
Come over here" . . . He points to the bath mat . . .
"Lie down on your back" . . . He shoves Johnny's knees

up . . . "Hold them there against your chest" . . . He squats with the bottle of Campho-Phenique . . . "Spread your legs apart so I can see what I'm doing . . . That's right" . . . He rubs the oil in Johnny's ass hairs and lightly around the rectum. Johnny sighs feeling the cold burn and looks down at his throbbing cock . . . "Like that Johnny?" . . . Mark takes a jar of mentholated Vaseline from the medicine cabinet. He rubs the Vaseline around Johnny's ass parting the soft pink flesh and shoves the middle finger all the way up vibrating the finger. Burning inside Johnny squirms and whimpers. His body pulls up his ass contracts spasmodically hot white spurts cover his thin stomach.

Feet twitching in the air shred to dust and memories pieces of legs and cocks and assholes drifting fragments falling softly through penny arcades and basement toilets playground finger stained with grass points to a red mark . . . "And there's another. Spread your legs" . . . Oh! Christ! it is happening a little whimper brings his finger up in three jerks blushes to his pounding heart looks down pointing naked boy on yellow toilet seat and later in Mexico City trying to remember who the stranger was in front of him ruffled brown hair blue eyes pants open far pale sun colored photo unbuttoned his shirt.

He looked at his young cousin just in from the country wondering if the boy would let him. They shared a room on the roof. They went to a movie that night and afterward in the roof room he got his cousin to smoke marijuana for the first time the boy laughing and rolling on the floor until he pissed in his pants sharp smell of urine in the Mexican night . . . "*Desnudate chico*" . . . The boy peeled off his wet pants and shorts and stood there naked and suddenly embarrassed under Kiki's knowing eyes. Then Kiki pulled him down on the bed tickling him in the ribs the boy laughing out of control . . . *"Por favor Kiki . . . Por favor"* . . . Trying to hide his hard-on turned over on his stomach Kiki straddled him and spread his ass cheeks and felt the body go limp under him and the boy said . . . *"Bueno, Kiki, haz' lo"* . . . Kiki put a pillow under the boy's crotch to get his ass up and spread the legs and greased the boy's ass panting and squirming as Kiki slid it in ten strokes and they came together in a red pull teeth bared cocks crowing in the summer night musky smell of the boy's greased ass.

Unexpected rising of the curtain can begin with the apartment building lonely young face in the hall standing under a dusty name . . . "Abrupt question brought me Mister" . . . Princes Arcade closing the lost past hung in his eyes boys and workshops pointing down the pale skies . . . "Through the dead I trust you" . . . The stairs stretched out a shadow. It was 6:40 P.M. Young face looking for a name hand holding the door open memory noises dim sky the lonely 1920 afternoon jerky bed twisted I remember the other straddles rectum palpable odor fills the room the past hangs in the air rubbish and weeds drift of time a child laughing blurred faces the dying sun through a bathroom window.

"Come over here Johnny. Down on your hands and knees. That's right. Spread your legs apart" . . . Cold burn on his rectum nuts aching Johnny sighs and looks down at his throbbing cock . . . "Like that Johnny?" . . . Mark gets a jar of mentholated Vaseline from the medicine cabinet rubbing it around pulling Johnny's ass open two greased fingers all the way up twisting burning Johnny spurts across the bath mat.

Buttocks dim trying to focus Johnny's ass the cold burn blankness a hotel on the outskirts of East St Louis. Johnny has just taken a shower. Flesh steaming he walks across the room to his suitcase. He takes out a package of Band-Aids and bends down to put one on a blister. Bending down like that it begins to get stiff between his legs. Mark is in an adjoining room and Johnny hopes he won't come in now but suddenly he knows that Mark is standing in the doorway and then he hears Mark's voice right behind him . . . "You look like a statue of Mercury Johnny. Why don't you stand up?" . . . Johnny blushes it is all the way up between his legs. Now Mark is in front of him. Johnny closes his knees looking up at Mark helplessly. Mark shoves him and he falls on his back legs in the air. Laughing Mark pries his legs apart naked boy hugging his knees sunlight in pubic hairs the two boys have been swimming they were standing naked arms around each other's shoulders looking at a redheaded woodpecker drumming on a persimmon tree sixty feet up in the summer sky. Suddenly Johnny began to feel uncomfortable with the other's arm around his shoulder. He shifted and glanced down Oh! Christ! it was happening he blushed bright red and the other boy smiled . . . "Your pecker's getting hard" . . . the woodpecker drumming frogs croaking the two boys were cousins but they had just met they were riding donkeys across the plateau and came to a stream under the bridge of an abandoned railroad the politicos stole all the money and then the railroad was built somewhere else rusty tracks overgrown with weeds and vines the older boy slid off his

donkey . . . *"Nadamos"* . . . The younger boy had a
hard-on from riding the donkey. Very slowly he took off
his shirt and shoved his pants down it was still half-up
he turned away to hide it. The older boy was already
naked . . . *"Qué te pasa chico?"* . . . The older boy
turned him around and laughed . . . *"Tú te empalmas"*
. . . In water up to the knees the older boy was wash-
ing his back slid the bar of soap down across his ass
something melted in his stomach and the other boy was
inside him. The sky dimmed out of focus as he came
hearing an ass bray from a great distance music across
the golf course the boy had been swimming in the pond
he sat on the concrete dam dangling his feet in the
water he got up dried himself and caught a gleam of
white in the summer twilight a golf ball he picked it
up and soon found another bending over to pick up the
ball he felt someone behind him he turned and an older
boy was standing there he recognized one of the town-
ies who hung out in front of Jake's Pool Hall the
boy smiled and walked toward him he stood there
feeling his nakedness under the knowing eyes the boy
stopped just in front of him . . . "What's your name?"
. . . "John" . . . the boy reached forward and cupped
his crotch . . . "Hello! Johnny" . . . the boy took
a deep breath and let's see you're sure the townie
stripped slowly turned him around with a quick knee
dropped him forward on hands and knees in the wet
grass finger rubbing something on his ass rectum spread
frogs croaking he was coming in a red pull through a
labyrinth of pink eggs sobbing gasps frogs in his head
the two bodies stuck together twitching feeling the soft
night air on his naked body two white balls in wet grass
I remember a thin pale boy last sad smile dust of dead
hope in his hands the proposition bleakly clear pointed

to the bed I remember hope of strange flesh the mouth dim room pants rip quick and silent coming another scene in the shed rubbish and weeds the drift of time a child's room pieces of a blurred face the dark city dying sun naked boy hugging his knees sunlight in pubic hairs sad muscle magazines over the florist shop corduroy pants down green snakes under rusty iron in the vacant lot the old family soap opera phosphorescent clock hands tick away to basement walls back yards and ash pits a silver crescent moon cuts the film sky machine-gun noises as he came one of the boys looks up hands mocking me off an old book with gilt edges the drawer stuck his distant hand there it is just to my shoulder twilight boy with violet eyes shredded to dust and memories paper fingers peanuts 1920 movie the old film stops A SILVER SMILE.

The
Frisco
Kid

Front Street Nome Alaska 1898. Across the street is
RESTAURANT. I walk through a path in waist-high
drifts past a dog team dog's breath in the air and open
the door of the restaurant smell of chop suey and chili
wood tables Chinese waiter. Order a bowl of chili and
coffee. There are several miners at the tables. I am
eating my chili when the door opens behind me and
icy air touches the back of my neck. Some one comes in
and sits down at my table. It is a young man about
twenty-three with very pale eyes. He says "Howdy"
and orders chop suey. There is talk from the other
tables of dogs and strikes and custom duties. I have
finished the chili. I am drinking coffee from a heavy
white mug with a chipped handle. The curtain between
the kitchen and the restaurant stirs as the waiter walks

back and forth. I get a whiff of opium. The Chinese
railroad workers are smoking in a room behind the
kitchen. The young man opposite me eats his chop suey.
He leans back in his chair and looks at me.

"Didn't I see you someplace?"

"Maybe. Where you from?"

"Frisco."

"I've been there once."

I offered him a cigarette. He took it fished a match out
of his pocket and lit it with a dirty fingernail. We both
inhaled deeply. The waiter set his coffee on the table.
The party of miners paid and left. We were alone in the
restaurant. I jerked a thumb toward the kitchen.

"Smoking. It keeps out the cold."

He just nodded looking at my face the eyes very pale
like I could see through them and out the back of his
head.

"They call me the Frisco Kid" he said.

"I'm Fred Flash from St Louis. Photographer."

"You got a place to stay?"

"No just got here."

"You can bunk with me then."

"All right."

He lived in a boarding house on a side street run by
Mrs Murphy.

"That will be two dollars extra per week" she said
when the Frisco Kid told her I would be sharing the
room. Room 18 on the third floor. He lit a kerosene
lamp. The room was lined with green-painted metal in
patterns of scrolls and flowers. There was a copper-
luster wash basin, a tarnished mirror, a double brass
bed, two chairs, a sea chest by the bed. The window
was narrow the cracks stuffed with quilting and cov-

ered by a frayed red curtain. We sat down on the bed
and lit cigarettes.

I get a whiff of me then I see room 18 wardrobe a
tarnished mirror the window him a cigarette quilting red curtains his fingernail the bed my face drifts
out of the back of his head he nodded coffee eating
my chili there was a door we went through and
some one comes in and sits down pale eyes chop
suey Mrs Murphy the room kerosene light his smile
through cigarette smoke. It was the first time I had seen
him smile. I lay back on the bed blowing smoke toward
the ceiling looking at the scrolls. Here and there a white
crust had formed streaked with rust. I yawned.

"I'd like to turn in if it's all right with you."

"Sure" he said. "Why waste money on some sucker
trap."

He stood up unbuttoning his shirt. He pulled off his
trousers. He turned back the bed and whiff of stale
flesh came off the blankets. We got in and lay there side
by side. He leaned over and blew out the lamp and the
smell of the wick hung in damp cold air of the room.
Outside angry voices from some saloon a distant pistol
shot. Then I was looking up at the ceiling and the room
was full of grey light, my breath hanging in the air. I
looked around at the lamp on the table the curtains the
window. It was very quiet outside muffled by snow. I
took in the clothes on pegs the wash stand the mirror. I
was lying on my back the Frisco Kid close beside me
one leg sprawled across my crotch. Under the leg my
cock was stiff and standing out of my shorts. I turned
and looked at him. His eyes were open in the grey milky
light and I felt a shiver down the spine. He wasn't there
really. Pale the picture was pale. I could see through

him. He smiled slow and rubbed his leg back and forth.
I sighed and moved with it. He brought his hands up
under the covers where I could see and made a fist and
shoved a finger in and out. I nodded. He put his hands
down and shoved his shorts off. I did the same. We lay
there side by side our breath hanging in the air. He
hitched an arm under my shoulders. With the other
hand he turned me on my side. He spit into his hand
and rubbed it on himself. Slow pressure I took a deep
breath and it slid all the way in. Ten strokes and we
came together shuddering gasps his breath on my back.
Where from? Frisco. A kid he never returns. In life used
young pale eyes. Lungs out and finished. Tarnished air
sunlight through the curtains red curtains his fingernail
smiled then and rubbed his leg.

"You someplace?"

"They call me the Frisco Kid. I'm out Front Street
Nome Alaska 1898."

"To stay?"

"No. Just got here. Want to."

I give you for that belated morning man about twenty-
three kerosene lamp on a sea chest. Smile through
me then I looked at room 18 been there might have
seen peeling my breath in the tarnished mirror someone
comes in and sits down my crotch feeling the ache in
my crotch stiff pulsing against his leg. Shoved his finger in and out I saw the fingernail shiny with dirt under
it. Shoved his shorts down we lay there side by side
naked he reached over and slid his hand down my
stomach and felt it tight and aching when I touched
him electric shiver same size same feel feeling myself.
Nodded "Sure"

He said "Why waste money on a whore?"

Turned back the bed and spit into his hand pressure I

breathe cold air the snow was drifting here and there
a white crust had formed on the window the wash stand
the mirror.

"Like to turn in if it's all right with you." Shoved his
shorts off stood there with nothing on stale flesh off the
blankets and felt it slide in silver flash behind the eyes
bright cold sunlight in the room every object sharp and
clear. I took in the clothes streaked with rust the ache
in my groin feeling a leg warm against it his pale smile
spit on my ass on my side facing the wall sliding in
tarnished sunlight I sighed and moved with it stiff he
opened his eyes and looked where I could see he wasn't
there really pale eyes looking down his leg.

"Call me the Frisco Kid. I'm out. Just got here. Want to."
Whiff of breath belated morning the Frisco Kid's legs
used out and finished pale. I could see through him my
cock was up under the covers he smiled finger in and
out going to turn me too smell peeling old places tarnished mirror shiver down my spine and through the
crotch a white crust had formed on his leg.

"If it's all right with you" and stood there with nothing
on the room was warm and I saw a wood stove. He
walked over and threw in a log and put a kettle on the
stove. He hung his coat on a wooden peg and I did the
same. He sat down on the bed and pulled his boots
off and I did the same. He took off his shirt and hung it
up pulled down his trousers. He took the kettle off the
stove and poured hot water in the copper-luster wash
basin. He rubbed soap over his face and neck and dried
himself standing in front of the mirror. He peeled off
his socks and there was a smell of feet and soap in the
room. He put the basin on the floor and washed his feet.
"Wash?"
"Sure."

He tossed me the towel and I dried myself.

"Warm in here" he said. He took off his long grey underwear matter of factly and hung it over his shirt. "If it's all right with you." He turned to me naked. He stood there and scratched his ass looking at me pale eyes touching me down my chest and stomach to the crotch and looking at him I could see his genitals were the same size and shape as mine he was seeing the same thing. We were standing a few feet apart looking at each other and I felt the blood rush to my crotch it was getting stiff I couldn't stop it his pale smile we stood there now both stiff looking at identical erections. We sat down on the edge of the bed. He made a fist and shoved his finger in and out. "That all right with you?" I nodded. He stood up and went to the wardrobe and came back with a tin of grease. He got on the bed and kneeled and made a motion with his hands pulling them in. I turned toward him on all fours he rubbed the grease in slow pressure and we were twisting he was pulling me up on my knees and shoving me down his hand on my eggs when I came there was a silver flash behind the eyes and I blacked out sort of there was a tarnished mirror over it stiff I looked at him his shorts stood out and I felt it naked.

"You figure to do?"

"I'm not here long."

Felt it tight and aching shiver down the spine.

"Why waste money on a whore?"

Shuddering gasps my groin shot pictures lawn streets sunlight faces a pale leg.

"Want to?"

Slow touching me down my chest genital smell peeling with nothing on the room was warm we stood there both stiff as wood.

In front of the basin and rubbed soap he turned to me and finished.

Rubbed his leg across my stomach to the crotch smiled finger in and out.

"All right with you?"

Getting stiff I couldn't stop it he peeled the bed "With you?" I nodded. "Just got here. Want to. Warm in here with you."

Shuddering off flash behind the eyes sunlight faces that's us all right in the mirror stiff standing by the wash basin wasn't there really. The Frisco Kid he never returns. In life used address I give you for that belated morning.

The
Penny Arcade
Peep Show

+ *""* Billy the Kid said: *"Quién es?"* Pat Garrett killed him. Jesse James said: "That picture's awful dusty." He got on a chair to dust off the death of Stonewall Jackson. Bob Ford killed him. Dutch Schultz said: "I want to pay. Let them leave me alone." He died two hours later without *saying anything else.*

+ *""* Sardine can cut open with scissors shoehorn has been used as spoon . . . dirty sock in a plate of moldy beans . . . toothpaste smear on wash stand glass . . . cigarette butt ground out in cold scrambled eggs . . .

+ *""* The old broken point of origin St Louis Missouri . . . lawn sprinklers summer golf course . . . iced tea and fried chicken at The Green Inn . . . classrooms silver stars . . . dust of young hand fading flickering thighs and buttocks made machine-gun noises as he came . . . "Look the Milky Way" . . . "But that was long ago and now my inspiration is in the stardust of the sky" . . . dim jerky faraway stars the drawer stuck his distant hand there it is just to my shoulder.

+ *" "* Wife waves as her husband takes off in an auto-giro. The sky is full of them. She gives orders to a robot that does the housework. In shattered cities muttering cripples pick through garbage.
"We set out Friday, April 23, 1976."
"June 25, 1988 Casablanca 4 P.M. A rundown sub-urban street."
"April 3, 1989 Marrakech . . . unlighted streets carriages with carbide lamps. It looks like an 1890 print from some explorer's travel book."

+ *" "* Clocks strike the hour. Seasons change. New Year revelers sing "Auld Lang Syne." Bell rings. Fighters go to their corners. Referee with stop watch ends soccer game.

+ *" "* Tissue, minerals, wood seen through electron microscope.

+ *" "* Stars and space seen through telescope.

+ *" "* Distant 1920 wind and dust.

The Dead Child

There is something special for me about golf courses something that is supposed to happen there. I remember the golf course in Tangier but it didn't happen there. I remember a room where the lights wouldn't turn on and later in Mexico City I see myself standing on a street under dusty trees, and through the trees and some telephone wires the Mexican sky so blue it hurts to look. I see myself streaking across the sky like a star to leave the earth forever. What holds me back? It is the bargain by which I am here at all. The bargain is this body that holds me here. I am fourteen years old a thin blond boy with pale blue eyes. My mind moves from one object to another in a series of blank factual stops. I am standing now in front of the country club. There is a doorman. I stand there until he no longer pays me any attention. If I stand somewhere long enough people stop looking at me and I can walk by them. People stop looking at me and then I can. The women in the market call me "*El Niño Muerto*" "*The Dead Child*" and cross themselves when I pass. I do not like the women young or old. I do not even like female animals and bitch dogs growl and whine at sight of me. I stand there under a dusty tree and wait. The members are walking in and out. Inside the gates is a building and beyond that the golf course. I want to get into the golf course but there is no hurry. A man sees me as he passes. He is looking not at me but around the edges drawing me out of the air. He stops and asks me if I want a sandwich. I tell him yes and he takes me inside where I sit at a table under vine trellises and he orders a sandwich and an orange drink.

(I buy the dead child a sandwich. An American boy here alone. Listen I made a wrong move finding that golf course to say sir and pretend to be the dead child. Way was blocked of course.)

The drink is very cold in my throat. I sit there and say nothing. There are several other men at the table. I can see the fuzzy word bits they call their "problems." I have no problems. I am supposed to reach the golf course to get into the golf course and through the trees. I remember a room beyond that golf course I want. A little shiny ball drifts out of my head and nudges the underside of the vine trellis like a balloon trying to fly up into the sky but a thin thread always holds it back. I am outside now. It is hot. The stranger has given me some money. There is a soda kiosk outside the gates where I buy another orange drink. Other orange drink. I am sleepy. I look around for a place to sleep. I find a corner where there are little round stones against the walls. Round stones are good to sleep on almost like sand. I make myself a place and leaning my knees against the wall fall asleep. When I wake up the stones are cool under my shirt. A man is standing over me. He is pink-faced and peevish. He asks me if I am a caddy. His caddy isn't here and he wants to know what kind of a club this is where he comes from clubs are run right. Yes I tell him I am a caddy. "Well then come along" he says. The doorman stops us. I am not a caddy of the club. The man argues. The doorman says we will have to clear it with the steward. Then we pass. The steward doesn't care. He gives me an armband with a little brass disk and number. I am 18. The man is not able to knock the ball far and can't see where it has gone. I find his balls for him right away. And he says I am the best caddy he ever had and what is an American boy doing here alone? I tell him I am an orphan which is a lie and he gives me twenty pesos. After the man has gone into the clubhouse I find my way blocked by several Mexican caddies.

"*Bueno, gringo . . . La plata.*"

Before my father started using morphine again he sent me to a Japanese person to learn something called Karate. I learn these things fast because I am blank inside, and I have no special way of moving or doing things so one way is the same to me as another. The Japanese man said I was the best student he ever had. He had a shower in his studio and in the shower he rubbed soap between my legs to look at what happens between my legs when a white juice spurts out. If I promised not to tell anyone he would teach me all the secrets he never showed other students. What happens between my legs is like a cold drink to me, it is just a feeling cold round stones against my back sunshine and shadow of Mexico. I know that other people think of it as something special to do with how they feel about someone else and there is a word love that means nothing to me at all. It is just a feeling between the legs, a sort of tingle.

The boy is there in front of me making a scene he saw in some movie. He is talking out of the corner of his mouth. He spits. I flip the back of my fist to his nose and blood spurts out. He covers his face and I punch him in the stomach. He falls down and lies there trying to get the air back. It is a long time coming and he is blue in the face before he can breathe again. When I come back next day a boy seventeen years old and nice to look at with white teeth and very red gums says that I am his pal and nobody will bother his pal. I am glad of that because what I am here for has nothing to do with that kind of fighting that dogs do and there is not much difference between people and dogs. I am not a person and I am not an animal. There is something I am here for something that I have to do before I can go. That day I caddy for an American colonel who tells me about keeping my eyes on the ball in life and on the golf course and life is a game and you have to keep your eyes on the ball and keeps telling me the ball is over here and when I find it over there he doesn't like it as if the ball should be where he thinks it is when the ball is someplace else. I am careful to say sir to him and pretend to listen, but I made a wrong move finding the balls too quick and he gives me a very small tip. After that I learn not to find the ball too quick and let the player think he has found it himself. And I get bigger tips and save the money. I don't like to go home. My father is taking morphine and always tying up his arm and talking to this old junky who has a government scrip and mother drinks tequila all day and there are kerosene heaters that smoke and the smell of kerosene in the cold blue morning. I rent a room near the club and stop going home at all. Now that I have more time to myself I can see what holds me back. It is not a thread like I thought a thin thread that holds a toy balloon a thread that might break and let me blow away across the sky. It is a net that is sometimes close around me and sometimes in the sky stretched between trees and telephone poles and buildings but always around me and I am always under it.

(Way is blocked beyond that golf course. Hands tingle. Morning legs in Mexico cool under my shirt. Standing there under a dusty tree hot white juice spurts out on the golf course. It is a feeling by which I am here at all.)

One afternoon I am in the shed where we change and take showers. The boy who said I was his pal is there. The others have gone because it is a fiesta. The boy has his shirt off and his skin is smooth like polished brown wood. He peels an orange and the smell of orange fills the shed. He breaks the orange in two and gives me half and pulls me down to sit beside him on the bench. He finishes the orange and licks his fingers. Then he puts his arms around my shoulders and I can see his pants are sticking up between his legs.

"*Yo muy caliente, Johnny.* Very hot." He rubs his face against mine. "*Quiero follarte.*"

His body is warm like an animal and I feel a soft tingle in my stomach and I say "*Muy bueno.*" We take off our clothes. The boy has two blue roses tattooed on each side of his rump. There is a musk smell from his tight brown nuts. He brings out a little tin of Vaseline he carries in his hip pocket because sometimes he would fuck a tourist for money he has always carried it. I take the tin and rub Vaseline on his cock feeling it jump in my hand like a frog he is standing there teeth bared gasping . . . *"Vuelvete y aganchete Johnny"* . . . I turn around and bend over hands braced on knees and let myself go limp inside as he slides it in I could see out through a little dusty window the golf course and the sun on the lake like bits of silver paper, and when I spurt the golf course seems to stretch out and then snap back pulling my eggs together and I am spurting out the trees and the grass and the lake. Silver spots boil in front of my eyes and the window blacks out.

I am sitting on the bench my head against the wall and he is rubbing a towel on my face. "You black out Johnny." He touched my cheek and looked at me showing the red gums and belched a smell of oranges. "You very good for fuck."

I don't remember. Maybe it didn't happen like that. One time we are swimming naked in the pond and afterward sitting on the dam. Behind the dam is a hollow place shaded by trees where the balls get lost and I lean back and see one down there through the leaves. I show him and we climb down. He gets there first and picks up the ball. *"Veya otra pelota."* He had found another. Squatting there he turned to me smiling holding a golf ball in each hand. Finding the balls has excited him and his eyes shine like an animal. We are completely hidden in a bowl of leaves. There is a smell of mud and moss and stagnant water. We squat there in the soft mud our knees touching. He looks down between his legs watching himself get stiff. He looks up smiling. *"Buen lugar para follar, Johnny."* I feel the tingle between my legs and I am getting stiff too. *"Esperate un momento."* He climbs up through the leaves and comes back with our clothes. He reaches in his pants pocket and brings out a little tin of Vaseline. He opens it and rubs it on himself kneeling. He motions with his hands pulling them in toward his crotch. *"Así Johnny."* I get down on my hands and knees feeling his finger inside me and my ass opens up and he is all the way in his hot quick breath on my back we shiver together and both finish in a few seconds. We sit there naked with our knees together and pass a cigarette back and forth. Then he opens his knees and shows me he is stiff again and says *"Otra vez Johnny."* This time he pulls me back between his legs and lies on his back with me on top of him kicking like a frog kicking the spurts out.

The sky stretched between my legs go limp as he slid it in afternoon I was in the shed boy had his shirt off legs together sitting on the bench he was rubbing he touched my cheek and looked and belched a smell of oranges sticking up between his legs rubbed his face against mine in the pond swimming naked treading water he puts his arm around me and pulled me against him *"Bailar Johnny?"* and I can feel him getting stiff against me. Then he floated on his back and it was sticking up in the sunlight we floated there side by side his arm around my shoulders. We swim over to the shallow water and he reaches up and gets his pants and takes the tin of Vaseline out of his pocket. The water is about three feet deep here and we are covered by the branches of a willow tree he kneels in

the green light the water reaches to his tight nuts. He
dries his prong with a handkerchief and rubs Vaseline
on it. "Stick your ass up Johnny." I raise myself out of
the water and he dries me with the handkerchief and
rubs the Vaseline inside. Then he hitches his hands
under my hips and pulls me up and my belly goes
loose under the water and it is inside me I am spurting
off into the cool water feeling his hot gobs inside. Afterward we stayed like that stuck together and inched
into a foot of water and I let myself sink down until
my belly was on the sand hollow place with bushes and
weeds where we took off our clothes squatting there I
could feel my nuts aching a little dusty window bits of
silver paper trees and grass the lake smell of oranges
pushed me down on my face he finished the orange
and licked his red shoulder *muy caliente* very hot
Johnny a boy animal knees touching stiff between his
legs sitting on the bench Johnny he touched in his pants
pocket and rubbed it his face against mine feeling his
finger feeling him get stiff he opened it sticking up in
the sunlight finished in a few seconds kicking *para follar*
my legs open *vuelvete y aganchete* Johnny I turned
stretched sky between my legs limp inside as he slid it
in legs go limp sun on the lake the golf course I spurted
off hot white juice silver spots in my eyes I remember
a room there naked musty smell of his tight nuts. I
don't know. Japanese person sometime. This me as another rubbed soap between my legs he would show me
what happens.

My room is on a roof. I can see blue mountains across
the valley. Every day after work Kiki comes to my room
and brings a packet of *griefa*. "*Muy bueno para follar
Johnny.*" We are sitting on the edge of the roof our

legs dangling in the air. I point to the sky above the blue mountains and tell him "Some day I will go away in that direction."

He looks at me and wrinkles his forehead like a dog and says I shouldn't think such things is *muy malo*. I can see he is sad feeling the sky between us.

Not long after that he was caddy for a rich Englishman and stopped coming to the club. I only saw him once after that. He drove to the club in a Jaguar car with new clothes and a big wrist watch. The clothes didn't look right on him. He was smiling but there was sadness and fear behind the eyes. He told me the man was taking him back to England. We shook hands and he drove away. At the end of the drive he turned and waved.

Stick your ass up Johnny few seconds kicking like a frog hands under my hips and pulled me up all the way in his face water and it was inside me stretched sky between my legs limp in the cool water we stayed like that stuck together I remember a little dusty room sometimes bits of silver paper child steps out of a shower feeling his tight nuts boy animal smiling he dried me hitched my legs open his hot gobs inside came there knees touching wrinkled his forehead like a dog sadness in his eyes waved good-by from his Jaguar.

What is it that makes a man a man and a cat a cat? It was broken there. It stretched and stretched and finally broke. Look at these broken fragments: centipede man, Jaguar man, limestone plant bursting out between his legs even the pain is no longer pain of man. This had started before I came there. I found the temple in ruins the stellae broken and no one knew any more how to use the calendar. Still the dead priests and their dead gods held us in a magic net and every day the overseer came from the ruined temple and told us what to do and for a while longer we did it in our minds and hands still heard still felt we could not do anything else. I was different from the others. I watched and waited. One day when the overseer came with his magic staff I raised my eyes and looked at him. I saw that his eyes were dead and there was no more power left in them. I knocked the staff out of his hands with my stone adze. He couldn't believe what had happened and stood there spitting pain pictures torture of the poison fish that turns the blood to screaming fire. I swung the adze up between his legs. He screamed and fell down thrashing around in the weeds and vines of the clearing. My friend Xolotl watched him and smiled. He stepped over and put a foot on the overseer's throat. Xolotl was holding a sharp planting stick. He folded one hand around it and with the other hand pumped it up and down between his legs like rubbing himself off making fire we call it and put out the overseer's eyes. Then he raised the stick and brought it down leaning his weight on it. The stick went right through the overseer's belly and pinned him to the ground. The others had gathered and stood in a circle watching. Xolotl got a burning stick from the fire and built a fire between the overseer's legs. After that we went to the temple. In a back room we found the old priestess like a paralyzed slug. We couldn't touch her because of the smell and a green slime over her body so we hooked vines around her and dragged her out into the clearing. She died before we could torture her. We burned the body. There were about thirty of us left five women and some babies that would not live long. Most of them had the terrible sickness from the old priestess that rots the bones inside. The legs go first they can't walk and crawl around like slugs then the spine and arms. Last of all the skull. Xolotl and I gathered our gourds and stone axes and knives and went into the jungle. We knew that if we stayed there we would catch the sickness. And I didn't want to stay where the women were. Xolotl and I went into the jungle where we lived by killing animals and catching fish. I can see the fish traps and the snares for delicate little jungle deer and animals that had a shell we could catch them with our hands and kill by bashing their heads against a tree. One time I smashed one of these gourd rats and the blood spurted out all over me. I threw him on the ground and he twisted around the sharp little black point between his legs was stiff. Xolotl laughed pointing to it then we were pointing to each other and laughing and I lay down pretending I was the gourd rat throwing myself around and Xolotl shoved my legs up and we made fire I was kicking like a frog. We lay there a long time until night came and it was cold on our bodies. Then we cooked the gourd rat in its shell scooping out the soft white meat. Next morning I looked around and decided this was a good place. There was a clear blue stream with deep pools and plenty of fish and a sand bank by the stream. So we made a clearing by burning the trees and built a hut there lashed to four great posts high above the ground. The biting flies do not come into a clear space. Fish were easy to catch with our traps and lines. And we snared deer and pigs and big rats and killed monkeys and animals that go upside down in trees with our bows and throwing sticks. But we did not kill the gourd rats after that. I knew it would be unlucky to do this. We ate and swam in the river and lay on the sand bank in the sun and made fire when we wanted. A lot of our time we spent making better bows and spears and knives. I found some very hard wood and made myself a long knife for cutting brush. It took me a long time to smooth the wood down with sand and when it was finished I could cut brush out of my way with it and once I killed a big snake with one blow. So I always carried this knife with me. We took animal skins and smoked them and rubbed the brains into the skins to make covers because it was cold at night and we used the brains to make fire together. One night I had a dream. A blue spirit came to me and showed me the vine where it lived and showed me how to cook the vine with other plants and make a medicine. The next day I found the vine and made the medicine like the spirit showed me. When it was dark I drank a little gourd of the medicine and gave a gourd to Xolotl. I felt the spirit come into me like soft blue fire and everything was blue. We got down on the ground growling and whining like animals. I climbed a tree and hung upside down from a branch. Xolotl was a jaguar, he pulled me down onto the sand I could hear myself whimpering my head bursting and flying away like stars that fall in the sky stretched the soft magic net when I spurted my insides out on the sand the blue spirit filled me Xolotl and I were part of the spirit and the vine where it lived growling and whining in my throat. We lay there on the sand bar and I saw places like the clearing where the temples were with many temples and huts and people green fields and lakes and little white balls flying through the air. When the medicine wore off we were very thirsty and went to the river and drank. Then we heard a jaguar in the jungle close by and went to the hut and covered ourselves with skins, we were shivering. The jaguar was always around after that we stayed in the hut at nights. We set snares and dug pits with spikes but we could never catch him, he was always out there grunting and snarling we could see his eyes shining in the dark. Xolotl had great fear of the jaguar. He would crawl whimpering into my arms like a child when he heard it outside sniffing around our hut. We took the vines but not often because it leaves a headache. I see the pot full of medicine on a slab of stone in the middle of the hut. Xolotl and I kneel naked in front of the pot. We dip out little gourds of the medicine and both drink it down. The medicine acts very fast. We are both stiff between the legs waiting for the spirit to come. Xolotl rubs animal brains on his fish. I lay down with my legs up and just as the spirit comes he slides the fish inside me, a blue fish swimming in my body swimming away into the sky where my head bursts spilling stars. I do it to him sometimes he is braced in the door of the hut head back whining in his throat as I swim into him I can feel my face in his and finally I feel my fish touch the tip of his and glow there with soft blue fire he is spurting into the night and the river the trees and birdcalls.

There was a full moon that night. I went to set out the fish traps and left Xolotl in the hut and told him not to go out. I have my wood knife with me if the jaguar jumps on me I will shove it right into his mouth. I find a deep silver pool and drop the trap into it. Then I hear the jaguar and screams from Xolotl. I run back to the clearing and there in front of the hut I see Xolotl on all fours. He tried to say something and a growl came instead his head twisted back by something is inside pulled his mouth open and teeth tore out dripping looking at me begging for help as the yellow light came from inside and put out his eyes and they shone green in the

moonlight and the jaguar was there twisting and throwing himself about growling whining spitting something
out his mouth a terrible black smell. My knife had fallen
and I was spitting up against a tree. For a long time I
was there against the tree the sharp smell of what I
had spit up in my mouth. Finally I pushed myself
away and got my knife. The jaguar had gone. Next day
I left the hut. I couldn't stay there. I walked in the
jungle and caught a few fish. Soon I was sick with
fever. The clay that holds a body together was broken.
Sometimes I was a tree or a rock and I would sit in one
place for light and dark hungry and thirsty. Sometimes
I took the vine and saw Xolotl solid I could touch almost and spoke to him but when he wasn't there I
didn't speak. After a while I couldn't eat and stopped
trying to catch anything. I left the river and walked
a few steps at a time came to a clearing and caught
my foot in some vines and fell down. I couldn't get up
the leg was broken there and I saw it was the clearing
where the temple was. I crawled to the edge of the
clearing under a tree. I crawled past the bones of the
overseer vines growing between his legs. The others
must all be dead. Soon I will be dead too. I lay there
under the tree and waited pictures in my head that
move and shift and go out and come back mixed with
smells and feeling and the taste of white meat and the
bitter vine and what I spit up from my stomach and I
was Xolotl. I saw that his eyes were dead jungle deer
and animals. I knock the staff out of the overseer's hand
with our hands. I throw the adze up between his legs.
He screams the sharp little black point stiff in weeds
and vines of the clearing laughed pointing pumped it
up fire we call it and put out our bodies. For a while
longer we did it in our jungle. I didn't want to stay

where the women watched and waited. I raised my eyes and looked at fish traps and snares. There was no more power left in them a shell my stone adze he couldn't there head against a tree spitting pain pictures to screaming fire. Xolotl throwing myself around and I was kicking rubbing off until night came and it was cold on our eyes. Making bets in the hut at night hard he was smooth I could see his eyes shining finished. A slab of brain to make fire together I kneel naked in front of the legs waiting for Xolotl rubs animal brains in my body on our hands and knees eggs bursting spilling stars animals growling and whining in the door of the hut between the legs I was stiff and I swim into him like a jaguar the head bursting glows in the sky soft spurts inside out on the sand he was spurting frogs and birdcalls there with my head against a tree it was night now and rain fell on my face and I held out my hands and caught enough to drink fish were easy to catch sand bar and I saw deer and little pigs kicking and squealing in the snares many temples and huts and people that go upside down in trees. I see the pot full of nights in the hut.

I lay down with my legs up to Xolotl. He slides the fish inside me and everything was blue swimming away into the sky and I did it to him sometimes he is Xolotl grabbed from behind head back whining in his throat could hear myself whimpering face in his out into the night stars glow there with soft blue fire when I squirted my river of running water and vines. Light and biting flies on my leg I couldn't feel them leg like wood except when I moved he screamed sharp fire it was broken limestone pain in animal's leg the dead around like birdcalls rain in my face I didn't want to stay I see the

pot and twisted hut. Xolotl, I had a dream my friend
Xolotl laughed on the overseer's throat Xolotl my legs
up to Xolotl kicking off into the sky. For a while longer
my head against a tree. I held out my hands no more
power left in them head against a tree it was cold on
my eyes moon that night solid I could touch almost
couldn't get the leg was broken and teeth tore past the
bones at me begging for help pictures all cut up knife
had fallen I lay there my pieces moved and shifted
against a tree I spit up from my stomach green when
day came and mist steamed up to the top of the high
tree just under the leaves at the top and looking down
I could see my body lying there the leg all twisted and
the face caved in lips drawn back showing teeth I could
see and hear but I couldn't talk without a throat without a tongue sun moon and stars on the face down
there worms in the leg weeds growing through the
bones. I stayed in the treetops. When I tried to get
above the trees something held me back I couldn't move
from the clearing to go above it or out to the sides.
Without words there is no time. I don't know how long
it was. Once some Indians came and built a big hut and
planted manioc and fished in the river. I came down to
watch them at night when the men did it with the
women in the hammocks I would get between their legs
feeling a soft net pulling me closer and closer. I knew
that if I got in the man's eggs and spurted into a
woman I would be helpless in the net. So I stayed away
up in the treetops. Or I tried to get close to the boys
and young men when they were away from the women.
Once by the river two boys were stiff laughing and
pointing to each other they made a line in the sand and
stood side by side and started rubbing themselves I got
close between their legs and one of them saw me and

screamed and the two boys ran back to the hut. An old man took the vine and said an evil spirit lived in the clearing. They went away and the hut fell in. After that I came down and lived in the cool stones and the vines rain sunshine a long time I was there I didn't go into the treetops any more because I knew I could not get above them and I didn't try to leave the clearing any more I stayed in stones and vines and tree trunks near the ground couldn't get any further feeling the net pulling me and teeth tearing through his gums I know that if I fear begging for help the women I will be helpless in the yellow light running into them the dead around like birdcalls helpless in the net rubbing himself and I got hands pumped it for a while my head saw me and screamed the bones at me begging for help under the stones and vines I could see my body lying there empty I couldn't talk without a throat the face down there worms in the leg twisted back
two boys
laughing off into the sky. I held out my hands. "NO." Ran back to the hut. Begging for something held me long long how long it was. Dust of the dead gods like cobwebs in the air.

Then pictures come that leave footprints. They come in boats with motors behind them. A man a woman a thin pale boy and six Indians with them. They have boxes and tools and hammocks and tents and set up their tents on the sand bar. The Indians clear away the trees in the old clearing and the man finds the ruined temple. They begin digging and bring out pots and flints and statues. The boy sleeps in a tent by himself. I was careful not to show myself at first. He fishes in the river and I follow him. Sometimes he turns around quick and looks behind him he can feel me there and I dodge into a tree. He goes and looks at the tree and walks around it and touches it. A full moon that night. I went to the boy's tent. Inside he was lying naked on his cot it was stiff between his legs he was rubbing himself. I was very close now between his legs he looked down and saw me there. He opened his mouth and I thought he might scream but he smiled and wriggled and went on rubbing himself wanting me to watch him do it. I got into his eggs squeezing through the soft tubes tighter tighter spurting gasping looking down at the hot white juice on my stomach seeing it through his eyes. I am the boy as a child lying naked on his underwear rubbing himself dust of the dead in his eyes. The pale skies fell apart. Suburban streets afternoon light bleakly clear rusting key. I left by the back door with the dust of a thousand years. I buy the dead child a sandwich. An American boy here alone. Listen I made a wrong move finding that golf course to say "sir" and pretend to be the dead child. Way was blocked of course.

Pilot lands there was his shadow . . . He was a caddy it seems . . . his smile across the golf course . . . sepia hair stirs in September wind . . . urine in narrow streets . . . slow finger . . . magazines . . . arched in gold letters solid boy out of the page . . . dim jerky his penis ejaculates . . . dawn smell of strange boy . . . naked thighs and buttocks . . . forgotten ribs rising on the bed . . . sepia picture boy getting browned on hands and knees in the wet grass knees stained distant lips parted.
Late visitor peculiar smile adroit gaze from object to object usually there was no difficulty. Does he know? "Dim in here" said the doctor . . . morning smell of the golf course . . . a ruin . . . pilot lands there was nuts . . .

dim shadow . . . vacant eyes . . . he was a caddy it seemed
stained with grass . . . water on the boy's legs . . . lean
boy by the pool . . . quivering legs in the blue morning
. . . feeling the sky rock . . . flickering dawn film stops
. . . transparent hands fading leaned down pointing
. . . "It's off." You see this? Couldn't find the micro-
waves . . . golf course . . . a ruin . . . Pilot lands there
in September wind . . . slow fingers touched his thighs
and buttocks . . . magazines . . . stained page . . . gasping feeling the cock up . . . transparent hand . . . laughing comparing movements . . . "Does he?" . . . morning
smell . . . sepia nuts . . . dawn wind between his legs
. . . dim shadow vacant eyes arched in gold letters . . .
distant lips twisted slow smile . . . the florist shop . . .
knees flickering . . . leaned down pointing . . . you know
this pain shifting outlines? You see this boy? Forgotten
ribs gasping . . . teeth bared . . . agony in his eyes . . .
pictures of war . . .

"Just Call Me Joe"

The American Crusade of 1976 . . . Chorus of youthful laughter and machine-gun noises . . . A medley of 1920 tunes . . . Boyish voices sing: "Meet me in St Louie Louie" . . . Flickering silver titles on screen . . . General Lewis Greenfield played by himself . . . Major William Bradshinkle played by Ishmael Cohen . . . The Mayor played by Green Tony . . . The CIA man played by Charles Ahearn . . . His two assistants played by Henry Coyne and Joe Rogers . . . The young lieutenant played by Jerry Wentworth . . . Wild boys played by native boys on locations . . .

A grimy red-brick building. National Guard Post 23 St Louis Missouri. Through a dusty barred window the gymnasium where businessmen in their middle and late thirties are learning Karate judo and commando tactics. The officers puff and lunge and throw each other awkwardly. Clearly some of them will require the services of a skilled osteopath in the foreseeable future. Vista of sagging bellies and fat buttocks in the locker room as the officers in various states of undress practice the holds . . . "No it works like this." Country club party table loaded with food and drinks. A guard officer has had one too many. He approaches a portly guest . . . "Bovard, I could kill you in twenty seconds . . . ten as a matter of fact . . . like this . . . I put my elbow against your Adam's apple throw a knee into your left kidney and bring the heel of my hand up sharp under your chin."

"Hey, what do you think you're doing?" The two men reel, lose balance and fall overturning the table of food. They roll around flailing at each other in a welter of lobster Newburgh, chicken salad, punch and baked Alaska.

"In the inland cities of America, men who are entering on middle age dream of a great task a great mission. They find a leader and a spokesman in General Lewis Greenfield."

General Greenfield on a white horse speaks from the top of Art Hill. He is a pompous red-faced man of fifty with a clipped white mustache.

Click of cameras.

"Over there." He points eastward with a statuesque arm. "Across the Atlantic is a sink of iniquity . . . A latter-day Sodom and Gomorrah. The reports compiled by our intelligence operators are difficult for decent people to believe" . . . Camera shows the CIA man, a tape recorder slung around his neck rests on his paunch. Naked youths flash on screen smoking hashish . . . "You

may say that what happens in a foreign land is no con-
cern of ours. But the vile tentacles of that evil are reaching into decent American homes" . . . Suburban couple
in the boy's room school banners on the wall. They are
reading a note

Dear Mom and Dad:.
I am going to join the wild boys. When you read this I
will be far away.

Johnny

"All over America kids like Johnny are deserting this
country and their great American heritage suborned by
the false promises of Moscow into a life of drugs and
vice. I say to you all that wherever anarchy, vice and
foul corruption rears the swollen hood of a cobra to
strike at everything we hold sacred, the very heart of
America is threatened. Can we stand idly by while our
youth, the very lifeblood of this great nation, drains
away into foreign sewers? Can we stand idly by while
the stench of corruption draws ever closer to our own
borders?" . . . Members of the audience cough and
cover their faces with handkerchiefs . . . "This plague
is spreading in every direction as deadly in its workings
as anything in the world. I am personally subscribing
ten million dollars for an expedition to crush the obscene thing once and for all."

"The press takes it up of course. National guard units
of every state in the union send officers and men.
Thousands of volunteers have to be turned away. Who
are these volunteers? Well I guess you could call them
plain ordinary American folk, decent tax-paying citizens
fed up with Godless anarchy and vice. You all know
the Wallace folks cop on the corner guy next door."

Scenes from World War I as the soldiers take leave of their loved ones.

"Over there over there over there
  The Yanks are coming the Yanks are coming
  And we won't come back till it's over over there"

Crap games on the troopship. The boys are glad to be away from their wives in an atmosphere of rough male camaraderie. Touch down at Casa red carpets, brass band, the Mayor there with keys of the city. Dinner for the officers in the Mayor's house. The Mayor speaks through an interpreter. "He say very glad Americans here. He say wild boys very bad cause much trouble. Police here not able do anything." As the interpreter talks plates are heaped with steak, catfish, turkey, mashed potatoes, ham and eggs, hominy grits, fried chicken, hush puppies, hog jowl and turnip greens all stacked on top of each other. The camera picks out a young captain.

"The young captain is thinking 'why these are good people like people in America are good. I guess good people are the same the world over, it's just as simple as that!' "

"He say after dinner when ladies go he tell you things what wild boy do. He say time for big cleanup. He say Americans like vacuum cleaner."

The interpreter bellows in imitation of a Hoover. The officers chuckle politely all except the CIA man and his two assistants who look sour and suspicious.

The ladies have left. "He say" . . . sound track cuts to silent film.

Music from "The Afternoon of a Faun." Nude youths smoking hashish. A runaway American boy is led in. He looks around and blushes bright red. A bare arm

passes him a hashish pipe. He smokes, coughs, then begins to laugh. Crazed by hashish he peels off his shirt.
He unbuckles his belt. "That's enough" says General
Greenfield gruffly pulling at his mustache. The officers
look at each other then look away in embarrassment
clearing their throats. They gulp brandy with one accord. Servants rush forward to fill the glasses which are
emptied again and again.

"Well I guess we know now what we're up against"
says the General huskily. "Jesus think of decent American kids . . . Why it could happen to your kid or
mine . . ."

Deeply moved the young captain excuses himself and
steps into the garden.

"He is proud of being an American. Proud of the decent
American thing he is doing. Why when he thinks of
those queers and dope freaks . . ."

A naked youth from the film appears in front of him.
He swings wildly at a privet hedge and cuts his hand
to the bone. He looks at his bloody hand.

"As we advance toward Marrakech cheering crowds
strew flowers in our path."

Cheering faces turn cold and blank behind American
backs. Cheering boys in this scene later appear in wild-
boy roles. Two English officers watch the parade. One
states flatly "They are the poorest excuse for soldiers
I have ever seen."

"Arriving in Marrakech we are met by the Mayor, a fat
smiling Italian."

"JUST CALL ME JOE" he says.

"He has put the officers' corps up in his villa. It makes
me uneasy the guards everywhere with tommy guns
looking us over."

The guards appear in shots from 1920 gangster films, black Cadillacs careening down city streets.

"And I can't tell him enough about my Eyetie buddies in the service, the one who got it in Vietnam I act it all out and die on the floor in my own arms taking both parts even the Eyeties were embarrassed but respectful too I'd outgroveled them one. Then we sit down to a good spaghetti dinner and I am telling the Mayor about Joe Garavelli's in St Louis spaghetti and roast-beef sandwiches after the skating rink."

The old broken point of origin St Louis Missouri. Mark and John, the Dib, Jimmy the Shrew, wild boys skating to old tunes and waltzes. The Blue Danube, Over the Waves, My Blue Heaven, Those Little White Lies, Stardust, What'll I Do with Just A Photograph To Remind Me of You, Tonight You Belong To Me, Meet Me In St Louie, Louie spinning lawn sprinklers, country clubs, summer golf courses, frogs in 1920 roads, cool basement toilets, a boy's twitching foot, the Varsity Drag, iced tea and fried chicken at The Green Inn, classrooms, silver stars, the old family soap opera . . . "When evening is nigh" . . . the dark city dying sun naked boy hugging his knees . . . "I hurry to my" . . . music across the golf course a crescent moon cuts the film sky . . . "blue heaven" . . . "The night that you told me" . . . decent people know they are right . . . "those little white lies" . . . White white white as far as the eye can see ahead a blinding flash of white fed up with Godless anarchy and corruption the cabin reeks of exploded stars. Made machine-gun noises as he came "Look the Milky Way" . . . "But that was long ago and now my inspiration is in the stardust of the sky" . . . dim jerky faraway stars the drawer stuck his distant hand

there it is just to my shoulder . . . "What'll I do when
you are far away" . . . far pale sun colored photo unbuttoned his shirt . . . "and I am blue" . . . colored photo
has something written on it . . . "What'll I do with
just a photograph" . . . "*Vuelvete y aganchete*" . . .
"to remind me of you" . . . trying to focus to remember
face on the grimy pillow . . . "If I had a talking picture
of you" . . . "Abrupt question brought me Mister" . . .
"I would play it every time I felt blue" . . . street
shadows in his eyes . . . "I would give ten shows a
day" . . . Mark squirms his shorts off . . . "and a midnight
matinee" . . . standing in the dark room the boy said
"I've come a long way" . . . "Oh! with the dawn I know
you'll be gone" . . . dust of young hand fading flickering
thighs and buttocks . . . "But tonight you belong to me"
. . . dawn shirt on the bed smell of young nights urine
in the gutter click of distant heels . . . "Meet me in St
Louie Louie" . . . The broken point of origin St Louis
Missouri muscle magazines over the florist shop pants
down sad old soap opera. Johnny steps into the shower.
Two boys turn with knowing smiles. What he sees
turns Johnny's face bright red feeling the red pull in
his groin sunsets freckles autumn leaves sun cold on a
thin boy with freckles silver paper in the wind frayed
sounds of a distant city. The boys are taking off their
skates. They go across the Street to Joe Garavelli's. Faraway spaghetti roast-beef sandwiches the camera stops
Joe's silver smile.

"You would have liked Joe" I am telling the Mayor.

Joe Garavelli and the Mayor sit at a kitchen table. Joe's
fat smiling wife brings up a bottle of red wine from the
cellar.

"Those tommy guns in the corridor aren't the only thing

makes me uneasy. It's Joe himself. I've seen him before."

Rome, Berlin, Naples, Saigon, Benghazi . . . "Here come
the Germans the Americans the English. Change the
welcome signs." Willkommen Deutschen is hastily taken
down and Hello! Johnny put up. "Sell your sister your
daughter your grandmother." Cigarettes chocolate and
K rations change hands.

"I have the uneasy feeling of being in someone else's
old film set. Yes I've seen Joe before. The smiling mouth
the cold treacherous eyes."
"We're going to win this war" I said quietly to a French
comte . . . (But loud enough so the CIA man can hear
me.) . . . *Le Comte* lifted his glass.
"I drink to the glorious victory of our brave American
allies over little boys armed with slingshots and scout
knives."
"I thought this was pretty nasty and told him America
was just doing a job we all knew had to be done and
we knew we were right and we knew we were going
to win, it was just as simple as that. *Le Comte* emitted
a sharp cold bray of laughter. Information as to the
number and disposition of enemy forces is vague and
contradictory."

The officers walk around passing out chocolate and
cigarettes. Boys point in various directions. These boys
appear later in wild-boy parts.

"They are somewhere to the south. All agree we have
only to show ourselves and the boys will surrender in
cheering crowds to escape their Russian and Chinese
slave drivers. This seems logical enough. None the less
we make careful plans for a military operation."

General Greenfield studying maps and pointing. "Just here is an old Foreign Legion fort. That should do for a base camp. Three days march from here."

"We set out Friday, April 23, 1976 the soldiers marching along singing 'Hinky Dinky Parlez Vous' and 'The Caissons Go Rolling Along.' The singing gets less and less lusty and finally stops altogether. It is evident the men are badly out of condition. It takes us six days to reach the fort. Three hundred yards from the fort the general holds up his hand and stops the column. All the officers whip out field glasses. The door is open three sand foxes sniffing around in the courtyard. They look up and see us and scamper off over a sand dune."

Fort from *Beau Geste*. Dry well thistles in the court-yard. The officers walk through empty rooms their foot-steps muted by sand. The walls give off a spectral smell of stale sweat. "This will do for the wardroom."

KILROY JACKED OFF HERE   B. J. MARTIN   D & D
     BUEN LUGAR PARA FOLLAR   QUIÉN ES?   A.D. KID

Phallic drawings . . . (Two Arab boys. One shoves a finger in and out his fist. The other nods. They pull off their jellabas.) Three American boy scouts look at the drawings . . . "Let's play, huh?"
"How you mean play?" says the third who is younger.
"We'll show you." Younger boy blushes and wets his lips as he sees what they are doing. Phallic shadows on a distant wall. Camera shifts hastily like embarrassed eyes. General Greenfield clears his throat and pulls at his mustache. "Sergeant!"
"Yes sir"
"Get a detail to clean this place out . . . and uh white-wash these walls."
"Yes sir."

"It is the General's plan to leave half our force in the fort select the youngest and fittest, proceed south and engage the enemy. He has named the fort Portland Place after a block in St Louis."

Two hours out of base camp several hundred boys waving white flags burst over a sand dune and rush toward us screaming.

"Hello! Johnny."

"You very good man."

"Thank you very much one cigarette."

"Chocolate."

"Corned bif."

"Americans very good peoples."

"Russians Chinese very bad." They snarl and spit.

"We show you where water is where make camp."

"Kif anything what you like."

"My sister she live near here."

Things seem to be working out. The boys will lead us to the Communist guerrillas who organize them and that will be that. The boys are vague as to the location of the guerrillas. "That way." They point south.

They find no water but demand extra rations for looking. Camping places they pick always seem to feature some particular inconvenience a nest of scorpions a cave full of snakes.

The boys rush around with sticks beating at the snakes knocking down tents upsetting pots of food stampeding the mules.

"The boys are under foot day and night and more of them keep surrendering. Must be a thousand of them now. Rations are becoming a problem. There is something about these boys that doesn't add up. I have a feeling that they are not young at all."

General Greenfield, the CIA man and Major Bradshinkle walk through the camp. Boys jump up in front
of them. "Hello! Johnny." The boys point and make
machine-gun noises. The CIA man looks at them with
cold disfavor. "Little bastards" he mutters.
"Just kids" says the General.
The CIA man grunts. "Something wrong here General.
They're not all that young."
As the officers turn away young eyes go cool and alert
looking after them with alien calculation.

"As a professional soldier I have the gravest reservations about the entire expedition. I keep these thoughts
to myself. A blacklisting from that CIA bastard could
mean the loss of my job. I think too much. Always have.
The security checks at West Point used to give me
headaches and I got the habit of taking codeine pills. I
have a good supply of pills I bought in Casa for the
chronic headache of this expedition. Not the first time
a bad habit saved a man's life."

A lunar photograph of shallow craters. "This Place of
Sand Fox. Good place to camp."
The CIA man looks around sourly. "I don't see any
sand foxes."
"Sand fox very shy. When you see sand fox nobody live
near."
As soon as camp is made the officers are summoned to
the General's tent.
Something has to be done about the boys.
The CIA man says they are obvious saboteurs smartest
thing would be to machine-gun the lot of them.
The Press Officer objects that such precipitate action
would jeopardize our public image.
"What public image? While you jokers were lapping up

booze and feeding your face Joe and Henry and me had a look around. They don't any of them like us one bit. That Mayor in Marrakech would cut your throat if you were down quick as he'd sell you his mother if you were on top. I tell you those brats are leading us straight into an ambush."

The General raises his hand for silence. "We will send the main body of boys back to base camp under guard retaining a few as guides. At the first hint of treachery we will radio base camp and the prisoners will be shot. This condition of course to be clearly impressed on the guides."

The CIA man grunted. "Well the sooner we get them under guard the better."

As we left the tent after receiving the General's decision about fifty boys came to meet us. "We got very important informations where base camp. *Muchos Chinos* there." The boys pull their eyes up at the corners yacking in false Chinese. The effect was irresistibly comic. Then the boys laughed. They laughed and laughed laughing *inside* us all the officers were laughing doubled over holding their guts in. The boys sneezed and coughed. They posted themselves in front of the CIA man and began to hiccup. He glared at them then hiccuped loudly again and again. It was happening all over the camp, a chorus of hiccups laughing, sneezing, coughing. The CIA man grabbed a megaphone and hiccuped out like a great frog: "Machine/hick/gun/hick/the little/hick/bastards!" And he reached for his forty-five. The boys dodged away. Wracked by hiccups his shots went wild killing two of our own men. The General grabbed the megaphone: "Men . . . ACHOO, ACHOO, ACHOO . . ."

"God bless you General ha! ha! ha!" said Rover Jones
one of his old yard nigras. Soldiers were rolling on the
ground pissing in their pants and then the boys were
on them with sticks knees feet and elbows. They
snatched up guns dodged behind some well-spaced
rocks and opened up at point-blank range. It was a
shambles. In a few seconds hundreds lay dead under a
withering fire from the boys. And the contagion was
spreading rapidly. One look at someone taken with the
fits and you have it. And the sneezes blow down wind
like tear gas. It is not just a ventriloquist act. It is a
trained killer virus. At least half the men were already
affected and those who weren't have been goofing off
somewhere survivors are all the goldbricks in this
stumblebum outfit. The CIA man caught a splash of
forty-five slugs right across his fat gut. He hiccuped a
rope of blood and went down like a sack of concrete.
The General was still on his feet trying to massa the
sneezes when a rifle bullet drilled him between the
eyes. He flopped on his face and bounced. In the im-
mortal words of Hemingway "the hole in the back of
his head where the bullet came out was big enough to
put your fist in if it was a small fist and you wanted to
put it there." I am in command. I begin to breathe
"heavy duty vast army ripped to shreds." I grab the
megaphone: "Keep your heads men. All who can walk
move out. Move out and take cover. If your buddies
have the laugh sneeze cough fits don't look at them,
don't go near them. Move out and take cover." The
wild boys stay hidden and pour it on. I lose a lot of men
before we get clear of the camp and take cover. Suddenly the boys stop shooting. I figure they are in the
camp grabbing all the guns and ammo they can carry.
After that they will move back and arm their con-

federates. Knowing how fast they can move over these rocks no use following with N.G. soldiers still blazing away at nothing. I give a cease fire. I doubt if the kids have lost a boy. Laughing, coughing, sneezing in the distance sounds like a congress of hyenas. Fifteen minutes and everything is quiet. The hiccups were the last to go. When we get back to camp not a man is left alive. Those who hadn't been shot had died from the fits, died spitting blood. It is a murderous biological weapon and I owe my immunity to God's Own Medicine. I turn the General over on his back and I will say one last thing for him he makes a fine-looking corpse. Burial is out of the question, too many stiffs. So I read the burial of the dead for morale and the bugler plays taps. We make camp a mile away. I am on the radio to base camp for reinforcements and medical supplies and *water* . . . "Art Hill calling Portland Place . . . Art Hill calling Portland Place . . . Come in please . . . Come in please . . ." I try for half an hour. Radio silence on Portland Place. From that point on I was looking out for Billy B., St Louis Encephalitis by birth and nickname.

"Save the water for those with a chance of making it." The young lieutenant gulps "Yes sir."

Quicker we get these stretcher cases off our back the better. They don't live long without water. Then we are hit by an epidemic of hepatitis the yellow sickness lives in straw the Arabs say and I remember the boys were always bringing us straw to sleep on. Hepatitis cases need bed rest and fruit juice. We are not in a condition to supply either one. When they got too weak to follow we left them there. It was the only thing to do worthless bastards and I hoped to make full colonel out of these slobs. The boys escort us with sniper fire deadly accurate keeping about three hundred yards behind us well spaced out. So we are pretty well thinned out by the time we sight base camp. There it is in the distance an old film set. We advance cautiously. Three hundred yards. I scan the fort through my field glasses. Nobody in sight. No flag. The door is open and I see three sand foxes sniffing around in the courtyard. We move slowly forward ready to take cover. Two hundred yards. One hundred yards. Fifty yards. We are standing in front of the fort now. It looks exactly as it looked when we arrived from Marrakech. Guns at the ready we move into the courtyard. Thistles the dry well. Nothing nobody. I take the young lieutenant and start a tour of the rooms. Sand on the floor silence, emptiness. It occurs to me I don't want a witness when I reach the wardroom in case any legal tender is lying about unliberated among other considerations. I turn to the lieutenant: "I'm going on alone, lieutenant. You go back and stay with the men. In case anything happens to me there must be a surviving officer."

He looks at me with deep admiration and says "Yes sir." God is he dumb.

The wardroom is empty.

KILROY JACKED OFF HERE   B. J. MARTIN   D & D
    BUEN LUGAR PARA FOLLAR   QUIÉN ES?   A.D. KID

I remember the man left in charge of the fort one Colonel Macintosh a druggist in civilian life. He was a huge heavy-boned man of a sluggish malignant disposition. And the horrible religious constipated captain who had been a prison psychologist in Texas. Captain Knowland if my memory serves.

KILROY JACKED OFF HERE   B. J. MARTIN   D & D
    BUEN LUGAR PARA FOLLAR   QUIÉN ES?   A.D. KID

No colonel no captain no desk no maps . . . nothing.
Empty room justlikethat. I feel a shiver in the back
of my neck as if a small animal with a cold nose has
just nuzzled me there. Even my memory picture of
those two jokers is dimming out. I can hardly see their
faces. Two people I disliked very much a long time ago,
so long I forget what they looked like. The colonel is
dissolving in front of my eyes to dust and shredded
memories where the old Macintosh Drug Store used to
be. What force could have moved that heavy-boned
lump of congealed hate? Perhaps something as simple
as a hiccup of time. Empty room justlikethat. Now I
know what the crusades are about. The young are an
alien species. They won't replace us by revolution. They
will forget and ignore us out of existence. Place of the
Sand Foxes was simply a casual entertainment with
just the right shade of show you. Leave us alone.
Leaning on the wall I scrawled a note. "Have been
ordered back to the flagship"

Colonel Macintosh

I walk back to the courtyard and show it to the lieutenant thanking God for his dumbness. He says "Well
at least they might have left us some water and pro-
visions." "Are you questioning the actions of a superior
officer lieutenant?" His Adam's apple bobs up and down
"Uh! no sir." "Good. Get the men on their feet. We're
moving out."

Dimming out I can hardly see one hundred yards. Field
glasses *mucho* long time ago. Thistles dry well another
species

Kilroy ordered back to flagship

Colonel Phallic Drawings

A sand fox sniffing the back of my neck. "Let's play,

Macintosh" . . . laughing hiccup of time. God is dumb. Long long radio silence on Portland Place.

"No water. More jaundice. Second day we sight a village, palm trees, a pool. I shout a warning over the megaphone but those I.Q. 80s rush straight into a fire hose of rifle- and machine-gun fire from the village. I pull back what's left. No use trying to take the village with the boys under cover. We skirt the village and go on. Of the 20,000 soldiers who set out under General Greenfield's command 1500 ragged yellow delirious survivors stagger into the American compound in Casa. (*Le Comte* emitted a sharp cold bray of laughter.) I am not with them. I know they will want someone to take the rap for this disaster and it isn't going to be me. And I know some nosy FBI bastard will want to know what happened to the payroll. I have a new name now and a nice business in Casa."

Joe Garavelli's restaurant in the suburbs of Casablanca. Wild Boys Welcome.

"JUST CALL ME JOE."

"Mother
and I
Would Like
to Know"

The uneasy spring of 1988. Under the pretext of drug
control suppressive police states have been set up
throughout the Western world. The precise program-
ing of thought feeling and apparent sensory impressions
by the technology outlined in bulletin 2332 enables the
police states to maintain a democratic façade from
behind which they loudly denounce as criminals, per-
verts and drug addicts anyone who opposes the control
machine. Underground armies operate in the large cities
enturbulating the police with false information through
anonymous phone calls and letters. Police with drawn
guns irrupt at the Senator's dinner party a very special
dinner party too that would tie up a sweet thing in
surplus planes.

"We been tipped off a nude reefer party is going on

here. Take the place apart boys and you folks keep your
clothes on or I'll blow your filthy guts out."
We put out false alarms on the police short wave direct-
ing patrol cars to nonexistent crimes and riots which
enables us to strike somewhere else. Squads of false
police search and beat the citizenry. False construction
workers tear up streets, rupture water mains, cut power
connections. Infra-sound installations set off every burglar alarm in the city. Our aim is total chaos.
Loft room map of the city on the wall. Fifty boys with
portable tape recorders record riots from TV. They are
dressed in identical grey flannel suits. They strap on
the recorders under gabardine topcoats and dust their
clothes lightly with tear gas. They hit the rush hour in
a flying wedge riot recordings on full blast police
whistles, screams, breaking glass crunch of nightsticks
tear gas flapping from their clothes. They scatter put on
press cards and come back to cover the action. Bearded
Yippies rush down a street with hammers breaking
every window on both sides leave a wake of screaming
burglar alarms strip off the beards, reverse collars and
they are fifty clean priests throwing petrol bombs under every car WHOOSH a block goes up behind them.
Some in fireman uniforms arrive with axes and hoses to
finish the good work.
In Mexico, South and Central America guerrilla units
are forming an army of liberation to free the United
States. In North Africa from Tangier to Timbuctu cor-
responding units prepare to liberate Western Europe
and the United Kingdom. Despite disparate aims and
personnel of its constituent members the underground
is agreed on basic objectives. We intend to march on
the police machine everywhere. We intend to destroy
the police machine and all its records. We intend to

destroy all dogmatic verbal systems. The family unit
and its cancerous expansion into tribes, countries, nations we will eradicate at its vegetable roots. We don't
want to hear any more family talk, mother talk, father
talk, cop talk, priest talk, country talk *or* party talk. To
put it country simple we have heard enough bullshit.

I am on my way from London to Tangier. In North
Africa I will contact the wild-boy packs that range
from the outskirts of Tangier to Timbuctu. Rotation
and exchange is a keystone of the underground. I am
bringing them modern weapons: laser guns, infra-sound
installations, Deadly Orgone Radiation. I will learn
their specialized skills and transfer wild-boy units to the
Western cities. We know that the West will invade
Africa and South America in an all-out attempt to crush
the guerrilla units. Doktor Kurt Unruh von Steinplatz,
in his four-volume treatise on the Authority Sickness,
predicts these latter-day crusades. We will be ready to
strike in their cities and to resist in the territories we
now hold. Meanwhile we watch and train and wait.

I have a thousand faces and a thousand names. I am
nobody I am everybody. I am me I am you. I am here
there forward back in out. I stay everywhere I stay no-
where. I stay present I stay absent.

Disguise is not a false beard dyed hair and plastic
surgery. Disguise is clothes and bearing and behavior
that leave no questions unanswered . . . American tourist with a wife he calls "Mother" . . . old queen on the
make . . . dirty beatnik . . . marginal film producer . . .
Every article of my luggage and clothing is carefully
planned to create a certain impression. Behind this
impression I can operate without interference for a
time. Just so long and long enough. So I walk down
Boulevard Pasteur handing out money to guides and

shoeshine boys. And that is only one of the civic things
I did. I bought one of those souvenir matchlocks clearly
destined to hang over a false fireplace in West Palm
Beach Florida, and I carried it around wrapped in
brown paper with the muzzle sticking out. I made
inquiries at the Consulate
"Now Mother and I would like to know."
And "MOTHER AND I WOULD LIKE TO KNOW"
in American Express and the Minzah pulling wads of
money out of my pocket "How much shall I give
them?" I asked the vice-consul for a horde of guides
had followed me into the Consulate. "I wonder if you've
met my congressman Joe Link?"
Nobody gets through my cover I assure you. There is no
better cover than a nuisance and a bore. When you see
my cover you don't look further. You look the other way
fast. For use on any foreign assignment there is nothing
like the old reliable American tourist cameras and light
meters slung all over him.
"How much shall I give him Mother?"
I can sidle up to any old bag she nods and smiles it's all
so familiar "must be that cute man we met on the plane
over from Gibraltar Captain Clark welcomes you aboard
and he says: 'Now what's this form? I don't read
Arabic.' Then he turns to me and says 'Mother I need
help.' And I show him how to fill out the form and after
that he would come up to me on the street this cute
man so helpless bobbing up everywhere."
"What is he saying Mother?"
"I think he wants money."
"They all do." He turns to an army of beggars, guides,
shoeshine boys and whores of all sexes and makes an
ineffectual gesture.
"Go away! Scram off!"

"One dirham Meester."

"One cigarette."

"You want beeg one Meester?"

And the old settlers pass on the other side. No they don't get through my cover. And I have a lot of special numbers for emergency use . . . Character with wild eyes that spin in little circles believes trepanning is the last answer pull you into a garage and try to do the job with an electric drill straightaway.

"Now if you'll kindly take a seat here."

"Say what is this?"

"All over in a minute and you'll be out of that rigid cranium."

So word goes out stay away from that one. You need him like a hole in the head. I have deadly old-style bores who are translating the Koran into Provençal or constructing a new cosmology based on "brain breathing." And the animal lover with exotic pets. The CIA man looks down with moist suspicious brow at the animal in his lap. It is a large ocelot its claws pricking into his flesh and every time he tries to shove it away the animal growls and digs in. I won't be seeing that Bay of Pigs again.

So I give myself a week on the build-up and make contact. Colonel Bradly knows the wild boys better than any man in Africa. In fact he has given his whole life to youth and it would seem gotten something back. There is talk of the devil's bargain and in fact he is indecently young-looking for a man of sixty odd. As the Colonel puts it with engaging candor: "The world is not my home you understand here on young people."

We have lunch on the terrace of his mountain house. A heavily wooded garden with pools and paths stretches down to a cliff over the sea. Lunch is turbot in cream sauce, grouse, wild asparagrass, peaches in wine. Quite a change from the grey cafeteria food I have been subjected to in Western cities where I pass myself off as one of the faceless apathetic citizens searched and questioned by the police on every corner, set upon by brazen muggers, stumbling home to my burglarized apartment to find the narcotics squad going through my medicine chest again. We are served by a lithe young Malay with bright red gums. Colonel Bradly jabs a fork at him.

"Had a job getting that dish through immigration. The Consulate wasn't at all helpful." After lunch we settle down to discuss my assignment.

"The wild boys are an overflow from North African cities that started in 1969. The uneasy spring of 1969 in Marrakech. Spring in Marrakech is always uneasy each day a little hotter knowing what Marrakech can be in August. That spring gasoline gangs prowled the rubbish heaps, alleys and squares of the city dousing just anybody with gasoline and setting that person on fire. They rush in anywhere nice young couple sitting in their chintzy middle-class living room when hello! yes hello! the gas boys rush in douse them head to foot with a pump fire extinguisher full of gasoline and I got some good pictures from a closet where I had prudently taken refuge. Shot of the boy who lit the match he let the rank and file slosh his couple then he lit a Swan match face young pure, pitiless as the cleansing fire brought the match close enough to catch the fumes. Then he lit a Player with the same match sucked the smoke in and smiled, he was listening to the screams and I thought My God what a cigarette ad: Clambake on a beach the BOY there with a match. He is looking at two girls in bikinis. As he lights the match they lean forward with a LUCKYSTRIKECHESTERFIELD-OLDGOLDCAMELPLAYER in the bim and give a pert little salute. The BOY turned out to be the hottest property in advertising. Enigmatic smile on the delicate young face. Just what is the BOY looking at? We had set out to sell cigarettes or whatever else we were paid to sell. The BOY was too hot to handle. Temples were erected to the BOY and there were posters of his face seventy feet high and all the teenagers began acting like the BOY looking at you with a dreamy look lips parted over their Wheaties. They all bought BOY shirts and BOY knives running around like wolf packs burning, looting, killing it spread everywhere all that summer in Marrakech the city would light up at night human torches flickering on walls, trees, fountains all very romantic you could map the dangerous areas sitting on your balcony under the stars sipping a Scotch. I looked across the square and watched a tourist burning in blue fire they had gasoline that burned in all colors by then . . . (He turned on the projector and stepped to the edge of the balcony) . . . Just look at them out there all those little figures dissolving in light. Rather like fairyland isn't it except for the smell of gasoline and burning flesh.

"Well they called in a strong man Colonel Arachnid Ben Driss who cruised the city in trucks rounded up the gas boys took them outside the walls shaved their heads and machine-gunned them. Survivors went underground or took to the deserts and the mountains where they evolved different ways of life and modes of combat."

The
Wild
Boys

"They have incredible stamina. A pack of wild boys can cover fifty miles a day. A handful of dates and a lump of brown sugar washed down with a cup of water keep them moving like that. The noise they make just before they charge . . . well I've seen it shatter a greenhouse fifty yards away. Let me show you what a wild-boy charge is like." He led the way into the projection room. "These are actual films of course but I have arranged them in narrative sequence. As you know I was with one of the first expeditionary forces sent out against the wild boys. Later I joined them. Seen the charges from both sides. Well here's one of my first films."

The Colonel reins in his horse. It is a bad spot. Steep hills slope down to a narrow dry river bed. He scans the hillsides carefully through his field glasses. The hills slope up to black mesas streaked with iron ore.

"Since our arrival in the territory the regiment had been feted by the local population who told us how glad they were the brave English soldiers had come to free them from the wild boys. The women and children pelted us with flowers in the street. It reeked of treachery but we were blinded by the terrible Bor Bor they were putting in our food and drink. Bor Bor is the drug of female illusion and it is said that he who takes Bor Bor cannot see a wild boy until it is too late.

"The regiment is well into the valley. It is a still hot afternoon with sullen electricity in the air. And suddenly there they are on both sides of us against the black mesas. The valley echos to their terrible charge cry a hissing outblast of breath like a vast WHOOO? . . . Their eyes light up inside like a cat's and their hair stands on end. And they charge down the slope with incredible speed leaping from side to side. We open up with everything we have and they still keep coming. They aren't human at all more like vicious little ghosts. They carry eighteen-inch bowie knives with knuckle-duster handles pouring into the river bed above and below us leaping down swinging their knives in the air. When one is killed a body is dragged aside and another takes his place. The regiment formed a square and it lasted about thirty seconds.

"I had prudently stashed my assets in a dry well where peering out through thistles I observed the carnage. I saw the Colonel empty his revolver and go down under ten wild boys. A moment later they tossed his bleeding head into the air and started a ball game. Just at dusk the wild boys got up and padded away. They left the bodies stripped to the skin many with the genitals cut off. The wild boys make little pouches from human testicles in which they carry their hashish and *khat*. The setting sun bathed the torn bodies in a pink glow. I walked happily about munching a chicken sandwich stopping now and again to observe an interesting cadaver.

"There are many groups scattered over a wide area from the outskirts of Tangier to the Blue Desert of Silence . . . glider boys with bows and laser guns, rollerskate boys—blue jockstraps and steel helmets, eighteen-inch bowie knives—naked blowgun boys long hair down their backs a kris at the thigh, slingshot boys, knife throwers, bowmen, bare-hand fighters, shaman boys who ride the wind and those who have control over snakes and dogs, boys skilled in bone-pointing and Juju magic who can stab the enemy reflected in a gourd of water, boys who call the locusts and the fleas, desert boys shy as little sand foxes, dream boys who see each other's dreams and the silent boys of the Blue Desert. Each group developed special skills and knowledge until it evolved into humanoid subspecies. One of the more spectacular units is the dreaded Warrior Ants made up of boys who have lost both hands in battle. They wear aluminum bikinis and sandals and tight steel helmets. They are attended by musicians and dancing boys, medical and electronic attendants who carry the weapons that are screwed into their stumps, buckle them into their bikinis, lace their sandals, wash and anoint their bodies with a musk of genitals, roses, carbolic soap, gardenias, jasmine, oil of cloves, ambergris and rectal mucus. This overpowering odor is the first warning of their presence. The smaller boys are equipped with razor-sharp pincers that can snip off a finger or sever a leg tendon. And they click their claws as they charge. The taller boys have long double-edged knives that can cut a scarf in the air screwed into both stumps."

On the screen the old regiment same canyon same Colonel. The Colonel sniffs uneasily. His horse rears and neighs. Suddenly there is a blast of silver light reflected from helmets knives and sandals. They hit the regiment like a whirlwind the ground ants cutting tendons, the shock troops slashing with both arms wade through the regiment heads floating in the air behind them. It is all over in a few seconds. Of the regiment there are no survivors. The wild boys take no prisoners. The first to receive attention were those so seriously wounded they could not live.

The Colonel paused and filled his kif pipe. He seemed to be looking at something far away and long ago and I flinched for I was a snippy Fulbright queen at the time dreading some distastefully intimate *experience* involving the amorous ghost of an Arab boy. What a bore he is with his tacky old Lawrence sets faithful native youths dying in his arms.

"As I have told you the first wild-boy tribes were fugitive survivors from the terror of Colonel Arachnid ben Driss. These boys in their early- and mid-teens had been swept into a whirlwind of riots, burning screams, machine guns and lifted out of time. Migrants of ape in gasoline crack of history. Officials denied that any repressive measures had followed nonexistent riots.

" 'There is no Colonel Arachnid in the Moroccan Army' said a spokesman for the Ministry of the Interior.

"No witnesses could be found who had noticed anything out of the ordinary other than the hottest August in many years. The gasoline boys and Colonel Arachnid were hallucinated by a drunken Reuters man who became temporarily deranged when his houseboy deserted him for an English pastry cook. I was myself the Reuters man as you may have gathered."

Here are the boys cooking over campfires . . . quiet valley by a stream calm young faces washed in the dawn before creation. The old phallic Gods of Greece and the assassins of Alamout still linger in the Moroccan hills like sad pilots waiting to pick up survivors. The piper's tune drifts down a St Louis street with the autumn leaves.

On screen an old book with gilt edges. Written in golden script *The Wild Boys*. A cold spring wind ruffles the pages.

Weather boys with clouds and rainbows and Northern lights in their eyes study the sky.

Glider boys ride a blue flash sunset on wings of pink and rose and gold laser guns shooting arrows of light.

Roller-skate boys turn slow circles in ruined suburbs China-blue half-moon in the morning sky.

Blue evening shadows in the old skating rink, smell of empty locker rooms and moldy jockstraps. A circle of boys sit on a gym mat hands clasped around the knees. The boys are naked except for blue steel helmets. Eyes move in a slow circle from crotch to crotch, silent, intent, they converge on one boy a thin dark youth his face spattered with adolescent pimples. He is getting stiff. He steps to the center of the circle and turns around three times. He sits down knees up facing the empty space in the circle where he sat. He pivots slowly looking at each boy in turn. His eyes lock with one boy. A fluid click a drop of lubricant squeezes out the tip of his phallus. He lies back his head on a leather cushion. The boy selected kneels in front of the other studying his genitals. He presses the tip open and looks at it through a lens of lubricant. He twists the tight nuts gently runs a slow precise finger up and down the shaft drawing lubricant along the divide line feeling for sensitive spots in the tip. The boy who is being masturbated rocks back hugging knees against his chest. The circle of boys sits silent lips parted watching faces calmed to razor sharpness. The boy quivers transparent suffused with blue light the pearly glands and delicate coral tracings of his backbone exposed.

A naked boy on perilous wings soars over a blue chasm. The air is full of wings . . . gliders launched from skis and sleds and skates, flying bicycles, sky-blue gliders with painted birds, an air schooner billowing white sails stabilized by autogiros. Boys climb in the rigging and wave from fragile decks.

Boy on a bicycle with autogiro wings sails off a precipice and floats slowly down into a valley of cobblestone streets and deep-blue canals. In a golf course sand pit hissing snake boys twist in slow copulations guarded by a ring of cobras.

The legend of the wild boys spread and boys from all over the world ran away to join them. Wild boys appeared in the mountains of Mexico, the jungles of South American and Southeastern Asia. Bandit country, guerrilla country, is wild-boy country. The wild boys exchange drugs, weapons, skills on a world-wide network. Some wild-boy tribes travel constantly taking the best cannabis seeds to the Amazon and bringing back cuttings of the Yage vine for the jungles of Southern Asia and Central Africa. Exchange of spells and potions. A common language based on variable transliteration of a simplified hieroglyphic script is spoken and written by

the wild boys. In remote dream rest areas the boys
fashion these glyphs from wood, metal, stone and
pottery. Each boy makes his own picture set. Sea chest
in an attic room, blue wallpaper ship scenes, copies of
Adventure and *Amazing Stories,* a .22 pump-action rifle
on the wall. A boy opens the chest and takes out the
words one by one ... The erect phallus which means in
wild-boy script as it does in Egyptian to stand before
or in the presence of, to confront to regard attentively
... a phallic statue of ebony with star sapphire eyes a
tiny opal set in the tip of the phallus ... two wooden
statues face each other in a yellow oak rocking chair.
The boy statues are covered with human skin tanned
in ambergris, carbolic soap, rose petals, rectal mucus,
smoked in hashish and burning leaves ... a yellow-haired
boy straddles a copper-skinned Mexican, feet braced
muscles carved in orgasm ... an alabaster boy lights up
blue inside, piper boy with a music box, roller-skate boy
of blue slate with a bowie knife in his hand, a post card
world of streams, freckled boy, blue outhouses covered
with morning glory- and rose vines where the boys jack
off on July afternoons shimmers in a Gysin painting ...
little peep shows ... flickering silver titles ... others
with colors and odors and raw naked flesh ... tight
nuts crinkle to autumn leaves ... blue chasms ... a
flight of birds. These word objects travel on the trade
routes from hand to hand. The wild boys see, touch,
taste, smell the words. Shrunken head of a CIA man
... a little twisted sentry his face cyanide blue ...
(A highly placed narcotics official tells a grim President: "The wild-boy thing is a cult based on drugs,
depravity and violence more dangerous than the hydro-
gen bomb.")
At a long work bench in the skating rink boys tinker

with tiny jet engines for their skates. They forge and
grind eighteen-inch bowie knives bolting on handles
of ebony and the ironwoods of South America that must
be worked with metal tools . . .
The roller-skate boys swerve down a wide palm-lined
avenue into a screaming blizzard of machine-gun bullets,
sun glinting on their knives and helmets, lips parted
eyes blazing. They slice through a patrol snatching
guns in the air.
Jungle work bench under a thatched roof . . . a ten-
foot blowgun with telescopic sights operated by com-
pressed air . . . tiny blowguns with darts no bigger
than a mosquito sting tipped with serum jaundice and
strange fevers . . .
In houseboats, basements, tents, tree houses, caves, and
lofts the wild boys fashion their weapons . . . a short
double-edged knife bolted to a strong spring whipped
back and forth slices to the bone . . . kris with a battery
vibrator in the handle . . . karate sticks . . . a knob of
ironwood protrudes between the first and second fingers and from each end of the fist . . . loaded gloves and
knuckle-dusters . . . crossbows and guns powered by
thick rubber sliced from an inner tube. These guns
shoot a lead slug fed in from a magazine above the
launching carriage. Quite accurate up to twenty yards
. . . a cyanide injector shaped like a pistol. The needle is
unscrewed from the end of the barrel, the pistol cocked
by drawing back a spring attached to the plunger. A
sponge soaked in cyanide solution is inserted, the
needle screwed back in place. When the trigger releases
the spring a massive dose of cyanide is squeezed into
the flesh causing instant death. When not in use the
needle is capped by a Buck Rogers Death Ray . . . cyanide darts and knives with hollow perforated blades

. . . a flintlock pistol loaded with crushed glass and cyanide crystals . . .

Cat boys fashion claws sewn into heavy leather gloves that are strapped around the wrist and forearm, the incurving hollow claws packed with cyanide paste. The boys in green jockstraps wait in a tree for the jungle patrol. They leap down on the soldiers, deadly claws slashing, digging in. Boys collect the weapons from twisted blue hands. They wash off blood and poison in a stream and pass around a kif pipe.

Snake boys in fish-skin jockstraps wade out of the bay. Each boy has a venomous speckled sea snake coiled around his arm. They move through scrub and palm to an electric fence that surrounds the officer's club. Through flowering shrubs Americans can be seen in the swimming pool blowing and puffing. The boys extend their arms through the fence index finger extended. The snakes drop off and glide toward the swimming pool.

A jungle patrol in Angola . . . suddenly black mambas streak down from trees on both sides of their path mouths open fangs striking necks and arms lashing up from the ground. Mamba boys black as obsidian with mamba-skin jockstraps and kris glide forward.

Five naked boys release cobras above a police post. As the snakes glide down the boys move their heads from side to side. Phalluses sway and stiffen. The boys snap their heads forward mouths open and ejaculate. Strangled cries from the police box. Faces impassive the boys wait until their erections subside.

Boys sweep a cloud of bubonic fleas like a net with tiny black knots into an enemy camp.

A baby- and semen black market flourished in the corrupt border cities, and we recruited male infants from birth. You could take your boy friend's sperm to

market, contact a broker who would arrange to inseminate medically inspected females. Nine months later
the male crop was taken to one of the remote peaceful
communes behind the front lines. A whole generation
arose that had never seen a woman's face nor heard a
woman's voice. In clandestine clinics fugitive technicians experimented with test-tube babies and cuttings.
Brad and Greg got out just under a "terminate with
extreme prejudice" order . . . And here is their clinic in
the Marshan Tangier. Laughing, comparing a line of
boys jack off into test tubes . . .

Here is a boy on his way to the cutting room. Brad and
Greg explain they are going to take a cutting from the
rectum very small and quite painless and the more
excited he is when they take the cutting better chance
there is that the cutting will *make* . . . They arrange
him on a table with his knees up rubber slings behind
the knees to keep him spread and turn an orgone funnel
on his ass and genitals. Then Brad slips a vibrating cutting tube up him. These are in hard rubber and plastic
perforated with pinpoint holes. Inside is a rotary knife
operated from the handle. When the ring expands it
forces bits of the lining through the holes which are
then clipped off by the knife.

Brad switches on the vibrator. The boy's pubic hairs
crackle with blue sparks, tight nuts pop egg-blue
worlds in air . . . Some boys red out rose-red delicate
sea-shell pinks come rainbows and Northern lights . . .
Here are fifty boys in one ward room, bent over hands
on knees, on all fours, legs up. Greg throws the master
switch. The boys writhe and squirm, leap about like
lemurs, eyes blazing blue chasms, semen pulsing sparks
of light. Little phantom figures dance on their bodies,

slide up and down their pulsing cocks, and ride the cutting tubes . . .

Little boy without a navel in a 1920 classroom. He places an apple on the teacher's desk

"I am giving you back your apple teacher."

He walks over to the blackboard and rubs out the word MOTHER.

Flanked by Brad and Greg he steps to the front of the stage and takes a bow to an audience of cheering boys eating peanuts and jacking off.

Now the cuttings are no longer needed. The boys create offspring known as Zimbus. Brad and Greg have retired to a remote YMCA. Zimbus are created after a battle when the forces of evil are in retreat . . .

The first to receive attention were those so seriously wounded that they could not live . . . A red-haired boy who had been shot through the liver was quickly stripped of bikini and sandals and propped up in a sitting position. Since they believe that the spirit leaves through the back of the head a recumbent position is considered unfavorable. The pack stood around the dying boy in a circle and a technician deftly removed the helmet. I saw then that the helmet was an intricate piece of electronic equipment. The technician took an eighteen-inch cylinder from a leather carrying case. The cylinder is made up of alternate layers of thin iron and human skin taken from the genitals of slain enemies. In the center of the cylinder is an iron tube which protrudes slightly from one end. The tube was brought within a few inches of the boy's wound. This has the effect of reducing pain or expediting the healing of a curable wound. Pain-killing drugs are never used since the cell-blanketing effect impedes departure of the spirit. Now a yoke was fitted over the boy's shoulders and what looked like a diving helmet was placed over his head. This helmet covered with leather on the outside is in two pieces one piece covering the front of the head the other the back. The technician made an adjustment and suddenly the back section shot back to the end of the yoke where it was caught and held by metal catches. Two sections are of magnetized iron inside the technician adjusting the direction of magnetic flow so that by a repelling action the two sections spring apart pushing the spirit out the back of the head. The flow is then reversed so that the two sections are pulling toward each other but held apart. This pulls the spirit out. A luminous haze like heat waves was quite visibly draining out the boy's head. The dancing boys who had gathered in a circle around the dying boy began playing their flutes a haunting melody of Pan pipes train whistles and lonely sidings as the haze shot up into the afternoon sky. The body went limp and the boy was dead. I saw this process repeated a number of times. When the dying had been separated from their bodies by this device those with curable wounds were treated. The cylinder was brought within an inch of the wound and moved up and down. I witnessed the miracle of almost immediate healing. A boy with a great gash in his thigh was soon hobbling about the wound looking as if it had been received some weeks before. The firearms were divided among the dancing boys and attendants. The boys busied themselves skinning the genitals of the slain soldiers pegging the skins out and rubbing in pastes and unguents for curing. They butchered the younger soldiers removing the heart and liver and bones for food and carted the cadavers some distance from the camp. These chores accomplished the boys spread out

rugs and lit hashish pipes. The warriors were stripped
by their attendants massaged and rubbed with musk.
The setting sun bathed their lean bodies in a red glow
as the boys gave way to an orgy of lust. Two boys
would take their place in the center of a rug and copu-
late to drums surrounded by a circle of silent naked
onlookers. I observed fifteen or twenty of these circles,
copulating couples standing, kneeling, on all fours,
faces rapt and empty. The odor of semen and rectal
mucus filled the air. When one couple finished another would take its place. No words were spoken only
the shuddering gasps and the pounding drums. A
yellow haze hovered over the quivering bodies as the
frenzied flesh dissolved in light. I noticed that a large
blue tent had been set up and that certain boys desig-
nated by the attendants retired to this tent and took
no part in the orgy. As the sun sank the exhausted
boys slept in naked heaps. The moon rose and boys
began to stir and light fires. Here and there hashish
pipes glowed. The smell of cooking meat drifted
through the air as the boys roasted the livers and
hearts of the slain soldiers and made broth from the
bones. Desert thistles shone silver in the moonlight. The
boys formed a circle in a natural amphitheater that
sloped down to a platform of sand. On this platform
they spread a round blue rug about eight feet in diameter. The four directions were indicated on this rug by
arrows and its position was checked against a compass.
The rug looked like a map crisscrossed with white lines
and shaded in striations of blue from the lightest egg
blue to blue black. The musicians formed an inner
circle around the rug playing on their flutes the haunting tune that had sped the dying on their way. Now one
of the boys who had taken no part in the recent orgy

stepped forward onto the rug. He stood there naked sniffing quivering head thrown back scanning the night sky. He stepped to the North and beckoned with both hands. He repeated the same gesture to the South East and West. I noticed that he had a tiny blue copy of the rug tattooed on each buttock. He knelt in the center of the rug studying the lines and patterns looking from the rug to his genitals. His phallus began to stir and stiffen. He leaned back until his face was turned to the sky. Slowly he raised both hands palms up and his hands drew a blue mist from the rug. He turned his hands over palms down and slowly lowered them pulling blue down from the sky. A pool of color swirled about his thighs. The mist ran into a vague shape as the color shifted from blue to pearly grey pink and finally red. A red being was now visible in front of the boy's body lying on his back knees up transparent thighs on either side of his flanks. The boy knelt there studying the red shape his eyes molding the body of a red-haired boy. Slowly he placed his hands behind knees that gave at his touch and moved them up to trembling ears of red smoke. A red boy was lying there buttocks spread the rectum a quivering rose that seemed to breathe, the body clearly outlined but still transparent. Slowly the boy penetrated the phantom body I could see his penis inside the other and as he moved in and out the soft red gelatin clung to his penis thighs and buttocks young skin taking shape legs in the air kicking spasmodically a red face on the rug lips parted the body always more solid. The boy leaned forward and fastened his lips to the other mouth spurting sperm inside and suddenly the red boy was solid buttocks quivering against the boy's groin as they breathed in and out of each other's lungs locked together the red body solid from the buttocks and penis to the twitching feet. They remained there quivering for thirty seconds. A red mist steamed off the red boy's body. I could see freckles and leg hairs. Slowly the boy withdrew his mouth. A red-haired boy lay there breathing deeply eyes closed. The boy withdrew his penis, straightened the red knees and lay the newborn Zimbu on his back. Now two attendants stepped forward with a litter of soft leather. Carefully they lifted the Zimbu onto the litter and carried him to the blue tent.

Another boy stepped onto the rug. He stood in the center of the rug and leaned forward hands on knees his eyes following the lines and patterns. His penis stiffened. He stood upright and walked to the four directions lifting his hands each time and saying one word I did not catch. A little wind sprang up that stirred the boy's pubic hairs and played over his body. He began to dance to the flutes and drums and as he danced a blue will-o'-the-wisp took shape in front of him shifting from one side of the rug to the other. The boy spread out his hands. The will-o'-the-wisp tried to dodge past but he caught it and brought his arms together pulling the blue shape against him. The color shifted from blue to pearly grey streaked with brown. His hands were stroking a naked flank and caressing a penis out of the air buttocks flattened against his body as he moved in fluid gyrations lips parted teeth bared. A brown body solid now ejaculated in shuddering gasps sperm hitting the rug left white streaks and spots that soaked into the crisscross of white lines. The boy held the Zimbu up pressing his chest in and out with his own breathing quivering to the blue tattoo. The Zimbu shuddered and ejaculated again. He hung limp in the other's arms. The attendants stepped forward with another litter. The Zimbu was carried away to the blue tent.

A boy with Mongoloid features steps onto the rug playing a flute to the four directions. As he plays phantom figures swirl around him taking shape out of moonlight, campfires and shadows. He kneels in the center of the rug playing his flute faster and faster. The shape of a boy on hands and knees is forming in front of him. He puts down his flute. His hands mold and knead the body in front of him pulling it against him with stroking movements that penetrate the pearly grey shape caressing it inside. The body shudders and quivers against him as he forms the buttocks around his penis stroking silver genitals out of the moonlight grey then pink and finally red the mouth parted in a gasp shuddering genitals out of the moon's haze a pale blond boy spurting thighs and buttocks and young skin. The flute player kneels there arms wrapped tightly around the Zimbu's chest breathing deeply until the Zimbu breathes with his own breathing quivering to the blue tattoo. The attendants step forward and carry the pale blond Zimbu to the blue tent.

A tall boy black as ebony steps onto the rug. He scans the sky. He walks around the rug three times. He walks back to the center of the rug. He brings both hands down and shakes his head. The music stops. The boys drift away.

It was explained to me that the ceremony I had just witnessed was performed after a battle in case any of the boys who had just been killed wished to return and that those who had lost their hands might wish to do since the body is born whole. However most of the spirits would have gone to the Blue Desert of Silence. They might want to return later and the wild boys made periodic expeditions to the Blue Desert. The Zimbus sleep in the blue tent. Picture in an old book with gilt edges. The picture is framed with roses intertwined . . . two bodies stuck together pale wraith of a blond boy lips parted full moon a circle of boys in silver helmets naked knees up. Under the picture in gold letters. Birth of a Zimbu. Boy with a flute charming a body out of the air. I turn the page. Boy with Mongoloid features is standing on a circular rug. He looks down at his stiffening phallus. A little wind stirs his pubic hairs. Buttocks tight curving inward at the bottom of the two craters a round blue tattoo miniature of the rug on which he stands. I turn the page. A boy is dancing will-o'-the-wisp dodges in front of him. I turn the page. Will-o'-the-wisp in his arms gathering outline luminous blue eyes trembling buttocks flattened against his body holding the Zimbu tight against his chest. His breathing serves as the Zimbu's lungs until his breathing is his own quivering to the blue tattoo children of lonely sidings, roses, afternoon sky. I turn the pages. Dawn shirt framed in roses dawn wind between his legs distant lips.

The
Penny Arcade
Peep Show

1. A copper coil going away pulling Audrey's flesh out in a stream of yellow light flash of showers buttocks soap you can see the hair on legs whispering phallic shadows in the locker room . . . "Wanta feel something nice Audrey?" . . . milky smell of phantom sperm.

2. Two copper coils going away peeling layers of old photos like dead skin . . . Tree house on a bluff over the valley. On closer inspection it is seen to be a reconstructed houseboat firmly moored between the branches of a giant oak and secured by anchor chains to an overhead branch. Branches swaying in the wind give the boat a slight roll. Standing at the wheel Audrey looks out across a post card valley stream winding by a village of brick houses and slate

roofs a distant train. Kiki the Mexican boy who lives down by the railroad tracks helped Audrey assemble the boat. There is a kitchen and shower. Often the boys spend weekends there. Kiki rolls cigarettes from a weed that grows along the tracks. Smoking these cigarettes makes Audrey laugh and get stiff at the same time. Flower smell of young hard-ons the two boys under the shower. Kiki kissed Audrey on the mouth and slid a soapy finger up his ass whispering the finger's question. After that Audrey used to bend over the wheel Kiki pumping him out across the afternoon sky.

3. Three copper coils going away . . . a red-haired boy called Pinkie came to live in the village. His father was a painter and the boy made sketches and water colors. Audrey has invited Pinkie up to the tree house to spend the night. Going up the ladder to the boat Kiki gooses Pinkie with his middle finger. The boy blushes and laughs nervously. In the boat the boys wash their dusty feet under the shower. They peel oranges and drink Whistle. Kiki passes around a weed cigarette. He squints at Pinkie through the smoke and asks an abrupt question. Pinkie looks down at his bare feet blushing . .

"Yeah. Sometimes."

"Is the hair around your dick red?"

"Sure."

"Take down your pants and show us."

"You guys too."

"You first."

"All right."

Pinkie takes off his shirt. Grinning he drops his pants and shorts and stands there flushed with excitement as his swaying cock stiffens. Kiki and Audrey strip. Sunlight in pubic hairs red black yellow. Kiki touches Pinkie's crotch with gentle precise fingers.

"Come up here and steer Pinkie." He leads Pinkie to the wheel. "Bend over and wrap your arms around it . . . That's right . . . spread your legs apart."

Trembling Pinkie obeys. As Audrey watches Kiki parts the buttocks rubbing Vaseline around the exposed rectum. Pinkie sighs deeply and his ass opens as if a pink mollusk had surfaced in the quivering flesh.

"All yours Audrey" . . . Audrey, his blue eyes shining, moves behind Pinkie Kiki would never let him this will be his first time can see the red ass hairs the soft flesh sucks him in playing with Pinkie's tight nuts running his finger lightly up and down the shaft Pinkie whimpers and wriggles against him Kiki's fingers prying Audrey's buttocks apart as Kiki squirms forward.

4. Four copper coils going away . . . Seen from above as a *Saturday Evening Post* cover . . . Pinkie waves to a distant train. Audrey laughed in the afternoon sky. Was a window of laughter shook the valley.

1. A copper coil coming in spatters Audrey's naked body with little bubbles of light that break and tingle his ass opens in a stream of yellow light laughter jumps phallic shadows sun licks flesh naked legs whispering light.

2. Two copper coils coming in . . . "Let's see you naked" . . . He licks his lips feeling the locker room pressure in his groin out of control knowing drops his pants and shorts swaying cock stiffens eyes shining sketches and water colors his ass opens a pink wheel soft clinging Audrey has him to the hilt.

3. Three copper coils coming in . . . "Didn't I see you at Webber's Post?" . . . Bleakly clear I am the boy as a child lying naked on his underwear rubbing himself my room and me there faded pink curtains yellow wallpaper three sketches. Flesh opens a silent door.

4. Four copper coils coming in . . . We're going to give you the last boy . . . yellow light late afternoon rubbing himself my room and me there dropped his pants and shorts eyes shining excitement . . . "Didn't I see you at Webber's Post?" . . . Bleakly clear I am the boy figure on the post card road faded down a street of memories blue light frayed sky . . . "You see this?" . . . Dim in on a stained silent door . . . "All yours Audrey" . . . tree house color pictures can see the red ass hairs buttocks carbolic soap in a stream down the shaft two boys laughing makes me think back child rubbing his pants pressure the swaying pink curtains and yellow wallpaper afternoon hills this whispering dust sea shells in an attic room face seen from a train maybe . . . the last boy.

The setting sun lights Audrey's dead burnt-out face.

Colonel Bradly advised me to contact the roller-skate and bicycle gangs operating in the suburbs of Casablanca.

"They are close enough to the regular guerrilla units so you can orient yourself. Through them you can arrange the special training necessary to contact the more inaccessible groups. Some of the wild boys do not talk at all. Others have developed cries, songs, words as weapons. Words that cut like buzz saws. Words that vibrate the entrails to jelly. Cold strange words that fall like icy nets on the mind. Virus words that eat the brain to muttering shreds. Idiot tunes that stick in the throat round and round night and day.

" 'here me is' 'HERE ME IS' 'here ME IS' 'HERE me is' 'HERE me IS' 'HERE ME is.' "

Ever hear the CIA talking baby talk? Ever see Narcotics Agents hula-hooping to idiot mambo? Ever seen a China Watcher clawing at the words in his throat? It gives you a funny feeling. You need special training to contact those boys . . . When you get to Casa go to the Cafe Azar on Niño Perdido where the old Fell Bridge Hotel used to be. The shoeshine boy is your contact there. He is known as the Dib."

Owing to the shortage of petrol there is no air service and very few cars on the ground. More primitive methods of transport have come back into use: stage coaches, balloons, camel- and mule trains, litters, rickshaws, covered wagons. There are a few steam railways in operation privately owned by the rich who live in feudal splendor on vast estates. When you want to travel you go to the Travel Pool a square surrounded by inns and brothels. You look around. There is always some way of getting where you want to go. Here is a steam truck that looks as if it will explode without more ado. I give it a wide berth. There are several obviously lethal rocket ships, a band of twenty Swedes with rucksacks on their way to the Atlas mountains, a mule train of guerrillas headed for Guillamine. A Commander with yachting cap supervises a lethargic Arab who is sewing patches on his balloon. "We've got a jolly good south wind coming up" he tells me. I decide to chance the Commander's balloon and settle down at a nearby inn for a long wait. About four in the afternoon his Arab wheels out a gas cylinder and by five the balloon is ready and we cast off. The balloon leaks audibly and the Commander reels about in the basket dead drunk smoking a cigar. The leak brings us down fifty miles north of Casa. I leave the Commander there and take a stage coach the rest of the way.

The Penny Arcade Peep Show

◀ The Chicago atomic scientists insist that the atom bomb should not be used under any circumstances.

▶ The atom bomb explodes over Hiroshima spreading radioactive particles.

◀ The old tycoon sat on a high balcony in a deck chair, his dark glasses glinting enigmatically in the afternoon sun. He was obsessed with immortality and spent vast sums on secret research. He didn't intend to share it with any groveling peasants. Serums, replacements of worn-out parts, were only a makeshift reprieve. He wanted more than that. He wanted to live forever. If the speed of light could be achieved or approached . . He was impatient with scientists who said this was impossible. "I don't pay them to tell me what they can't do . . . Why a rocket with enough push behind it . . ." He did not like to hear the word DEATH spoken in his presence and suddenly boyish voices were singing "The worms crawl in and the worms crawl out."

He looked up to see a fleet of gliders drifting toward him on the afternoon wind piloted by youths in skeleton suits. Silver arrows rained from the sky.

▶ Audrey was in an Eastern market. Steep wooden ramps sloped dizzily down like a roller coaster lined with fruit-and-vegetable stalls. He was sitting at the wheel of a heavy wooden cart with iron wheels and bumper. The cart picked up speed, crashing into stalls, spilling fruit and vegetables which rolled down the ramp. Dogs and chickens and children scattered out from under his wheels "I don't care who I run into" he thought. He was possessed by an ugly spirit of destroying speed. He caught sight of a large cobra by the side of the ramp and swerved to run over it. Writhing fragments flew up in his face. He screamed.

◀ Armored cars, sirens screaming converge on a rocket installation.

▶ Too late. The rocket blasts off a mad tycoon at the controls. The earth blows up behind him. As his ship rides the blast he screams: "HI HO SILVER YIPPEEE." He is riding ahead of a posse tossing sticks of dynamite over his shoulder. Sharp smell of weeds from old Westerns.

◀ House of the General city of Resht in Northern Persia 1023 A.D. The General is poring over maps as he plans an expedition against Alamout. The Old Man of the Mountain represented for the General

pure demonic evil. Certainly this man had com-
mitted the terrible sin referred to in the Koran of
aspiring to be God. The whole Ishmaelian sect was a
perfect curse, hidden, lurking, ready to strike, defy-
ing all authority . . . "Nothing is true. Everything is
permitted."

"Blasphemy" the General screamed starting to his
feet. "Man is made to submit and obey."

Acting out a final confrontation with this Satan he
paces the room fingering the jeweled handle of his
sword. He cannot return to his maps. Still muttering
imprecations he steps into the garden. Under the
orange trees an old man is cutting weeds stopping
from time to time to hone his knife on a stone, hands
like brown silk unhurried and steady. He has worked
there as a gardener for ten years and the General has
stopped seeing him years ago. He is as much a part
of the garden as the orange trees and the irrigation
ditch flashing like a sword in sun. The House of the
General is built on a high hill. Orange groves, date
palms, rosebushes, pools and opium poppies stretch
down to massive walls. The Caspian Sea gleams in
the distance. But the General can find no peace in
his garden today. The Old Man peers at this through
the orange leaves with laughing blue eyes and stabs
up at him from the irrigation ditch. Forgetting the
presence of his servant the General raises his
clenched fist to a distant mountain and screams:
"Satan, I will destroy you forever."

▶ Squatting in front of the sharpening stone the old
gardener tests the edge of his blade against his
thumb. The old gardener tested the edge of ten years
unhurried eyes seeing the General long ago in a blaze

of white light. He straightens up with all the power of his bent knees thrusting up under the rib cage knife seeking a distant point beyond the general's sagging body, HIS knife flashing like a compass needle straight from Alamout.

The
Wild
Boys
Smile

June 25, 1988 Casablanca 4 P.M. The Café Azar was on
a rundown suburban street you could find in Fort
Worth Texas. CAFÉ AZAR in red letters on plate glass
the interior hidden from the street by faded pink curtains. Inside a few Europeans and Arabs drinking tea
and soft drinks. The shoeshine boy came over and
pointed to my shoes. He was naked except for a dirty
white jockstrap and leather sandals. His head was
shaved and a tuft of hair sprouted from the crown. His
face had been beautiful at some other time and place
now broken and twisted by altered pressure, the teeth
stuck out at angles features wrenched out of focus body
emaciated by distant hungers. He sat on his box and
looked up at me squinting snub-nosed legs sprawled

apart one finger scratching his jock. The skin was white
as paper hairs black and shiny lay flat on his skinny legs.
As he shined my shoes with deft precise movements his
body gave off a dry musty smell. In one corner of the
room I saw a green curtain in front of which two boys
were undressing. The corner was apparently at a level
below the café floor since I could not see their legs
below the knee. One of the boys had stripped to pink
underwear sticking out straight at the fly. The other
patrons paid no attention to this tableau. The boy
jerked his head toward the two actors who were now
fucking in upright position lips parted in silent gasps.
He put a finger to one eye and shook his head. The
others could not see the boys. I handed the boy a coin.
He checked the date and nodded. The Dib checked the
date of nettles feet twisted by the altered disk.
"Long time nobody use jump" he said leg hairs covered
with mold. The gun jumping, crumpled twisted body,
his face floating there the soldier's identification card
and skinny in picture.
"I was too." He pointed to his thin body. He picked up
his box. I followed him through the cafe. When I walk
with the Dib they can't see me. Buttocks were smooth
and white as old ivory. The corner of the green curtain
was a sunken limestone square two steps down from the
café floor dry musty smell of empty waiting rooms a
worn wood bench along one wall. Embedded in the
stone floor was an iron disk about five feet in diameter
degrees and numbers cut in its edges brass arrows indicating N. S. E. W. This compass floated on a hydraulic
medium. In the center of the disk a marine compass
occupied a teakwood socket. Two pairs of sandals worn
smooth and black mounted on spring stilts eight inches

in height were spaced eighteen inches apart so that two people standing in the sandals would be one behind the other the center of the disk and the marine compass exactly between them. The springs were bolted to pistons which projected on shafts from the iron disk. The sandals were at different levels. Evidently they could be adjusted by raising or lowering the shafts. At a sign from the boy I stripped off my clothes smooth hands guided by film tracks I was to bend over and brace my hands on my knees. The boy reached in his box and took out a tape measure that ended in a little knob. He measured the distance from my rectum to the floor. With a round key which fitted into locks in the support shafts he adjusted the level of the two pairs of sandals on the spring stilts. He stood up and stripped off his jockstrap scraping erection. He mounted one pair of spring stilts and strapped his feet into the sandals poised on the springs nuts tight and precise as bearings his phallus projected needle of the compass the disk turned until it was facing the green curtain which moved slightly as if it might cover an opening, ass arrows indicating N. S. E. W. feet a taste of metal in the mouth 18 penis floated I stepped in the sandals from behind knees his skinny arms and I was seeing the take from outside at different levels soft machine my ass a rusty cylinder pearly glands electric click blue sparks my spine into his I bend over and brace vibrating on the springs iron smell of rectal mucus streaking across the sky a wrench spurting soft tracks a distant gun jumping the soldier's identification disk covered with mold his smile across tears of pain squinting up at me snub-nosed hands at the crotch worn metal smell of the gun as my feet touched the iron disk a soft shock tingled up my legs to the crotch. The penis floated. I

stepped onto the stilts in front of the boy and he adjusted the straps from behind. I bent over and braced
my hands on my knees. He hooked his skinny arms
under my shoulders leg hairs twisted together a slow
greased pressure and I was seeing the take from outside transparent soft machine ass a rusty cylinder phallus a piston pumping the pearly glands blue sparks and
my spine clicked back into his then forward his head
in mine eyes steering through a maze of turnstiles. Stop.
Click. Start. Stop. Click. Start streaking across the sky
a smear of pain gun jumping out trees weed-grown
tracks rusty identification disk covered with mold.
Click. Green Pullman curtain. Click. "You wanta see
something?" Click. Penis floated. Click. Distant 1920
wind and dust. Click. Bits of silver paper in a wind
across the park. Click. Summer afternoon on car seat to
the thin brown knees. Click. His smile across the golf
course. Click. Click. Click. See on back what I mean each
time place dim jerky faraway. The curtain stirs slightly.
Click. Sharp smell of weeds. The curtain was gone. The
feeling in my stomach when a fast elevator stops as
we landed in a stone kiosk by an abandoned railroad
dried shit urine initials

KILROY JACKED OFF HERE   B. J. MARTIN   D & D
    BUEN LUGAR PARA FOLLAR   QUIÉN ES?   A.D. KID

We unlaced our feet and stepped down from the
springs. The disk was rusty and rust had stained the
stone around its edges.
"Long time nobody use jump" the boy said pointing. I
saw my clothes in a corner covered with mold. The boy
shook his head and handed me a white jockstrap from
his box.
"Clothes no good here. Easy see clothes. Very hard see

this." He pointed to his thin body.

Then I felt the thirst my body dry and brittle as a dead leaf.

"Jump take your last water Meester. We find spring."

Above the kiosk was a steep hillside. The boy made his way through brush that seemed to move aside for him leaving a tunnel of leaves. He dropped on his knees and parted a tangle of vines. A deep black spring flowed from a limestone cleft. We scooped up clear cold water with our hands. The boy wiped his mouth. From the hillside we could see a railroad bridge, a stream, ruined suburbs.

"This bad place Meester. Patrols out here."

The boy reached into his box and brought out two packages of oiled paper tied with cord. He undid the cord and unwrapped two snub-nosed thirty-eight re-volvers the hammers filed off, the grips cut short, the checked walnut stocks worn smooth. The revolvers could only be used double action. The grip came to the middle of my palm held precisely in place by two con-verging mounds of hard flesh like part of my hand. The boy pointed with his revolver indicating the path we were going to take into the town under the bridge along the stream. There was no sign of life in the town ruined villas overgrown with vines empty cafés and courtyards. The boy led the way. He would move for-ward in a burst of speed for fifty feet or so then stop poised sniffing quivering. We were walking along a path by a white wall.

"DOWN MEESTER!"

A burst of machine-gun fire ripped into the wall. I threw myself into a ditch full of nettles. Pain poured out my arm like a fire hose gun jumping. Three soldiers about forty feet away crumpled twisted and fell. The boy got up blowing smoke from his gun barrel body covered with red welts. In a burst of speed his feet reached the bodies. I had fired twice. He had fired four times. Every bullet had found a vital spot. One soldier lay on his back legs twisted under him a hole in the middle of his forehead. Another was still alive twitching convulsively as blood spurted from a neck wound. The third had been shot three times in the stomach. He lay face down hands clasped over his stomach, his machine gun still smoking three yards away white smoke curling up from the grass. It was a subdivision street, lawns, palm trees, bungalows built along one side vacant lot opposite could have been Palm Beach Florida empty ten years weeds palm branches in the driveways, windows broken, no sign of life. The boy went through pockets with expert fingers: a knife, identification papers, cigarettes, a packet of kif. Two of the soldiers had been carrying carbines the third a submachine gun. "No good Czech grease gun" the boy said and kicked it aside after unclipping the magazine. The carbines he propped against a palm tree. We dragged the bodies into a ditch. The pressure of pain lent maniac power and precision to our movements. We rushed about dragging palm branches to heap on the bodies. We couldn't stop. We found a Christmas tree bits of silver paper twisted in its brown needles and heaved it over onto the dead soldiers. We paused panting shivering and looked at each other. Spots boiled in front of my eyes blood pounded to neck and crotch feeling the strap tighten hot squeezing pressure inside stomach intestines a muffled explosion as scalding diarrhea spurted down the backs of our trembling thighs the Boy Scout Manual floated across summer afternoons the boy's cracked broken film voice seeing the take from outside the shelf I rummaged

in the shelf knew what I was looking for along a flagstone path feet like blocks of wood trailing black oily
shit this must be the kitchen door open rusty electric
stove moldy chili dishes food containers silver paper
knew what I was looking for rummaged in the shelves
fingers numb wet-dream tension in my crotch and I
knew there was not much time found a can of baking
powder emptied it into a porcelain fruit bowl painted
roses no water silver pies choking in a red haze not
much time out into the ruined garden fish pond stagnant water green slime a frog jumped the boy was tearing at his jockstrap I sat down and slipped my strap
off strap halfway down his thighs cock flipped out stiff
he lost balance fell on his side I pulled the strap down
off his feet he turned on his back knees up body arched
pulled together spurted neck tumescent choking I
dipped water and green slime into the bowl with both
hands mixed a paste slapped the paste on both sides of
his neck and down the chest to the heart ejaculated
across his quivering stomach I dipped more paste held
it to the sides of my throbbing neck then down the
chest I could breathe now easier to move more paste
down the boy's stomach and thighs to the feet turned
him over and rubbed the paste down his back where
the nettles had whipped great welts across the back he
sighed simpered body went limp and emptied again. I
stood up and rubbed the paste over my body the pain
was going and the numbness. I flopped down beside
the boy and fell into a deep sleep.

"Five Indian youths accompanied us from the village in
the capacity of guides. Actually they seemed quite
ignorant of the country we were traversing and spent
much of their time hunting with an old muzzle-loading

shotgun more hazardous to the hunters than the quarry. Five days out of Candiru in the head waters of the Babboonsasshole, they managed to wound a deer. Chasing the wounded animal in wild excitement they ran through a patch of nettles. They emerged covered from head to foot with pulsing welts whipped across red skins like dusky roses. Fortunately they were wearing loincloths. Pain seemed to lend fleetness and energy to the pursuit and they brought the deer down with another shot. They closed on the dying animal with shrill cries of triumph and severed its head with a machete. Quite suddenly they were silent looking at each other and with one accord were seized by uncontrollable diarrhea. They tore off their loincloths in a frenzy of lust, faces tumescent eyes swollen shut, threw themselves on the ground ejaculating and defecating again and again. We watched powerless to aid them until the Chinese cook with rare presence of mind mixed baking powder into a thick paste with water. He applied this paste to the neck of the nearest youth and then down the chest to the heart. In this way he was able to save two of the youths but the other three perished in erotic convulsions. As to whether the nettles were of a special variety or the symptoms resulted from an excess of formic acid circulated through the blood by exertion I could not say. The prompt relief afforded by applying an alkaline paste would suggest that the symptoms resulted from some form of acid poisoning." Quote Greenbaum early explorer.

When we woke up the sun was setting. We were smeared with a dried paste of shit, baking powder and green slime as if anointed for some ceremony or sacrifice. We found soap in the kitchen and washed off the crusted paste feeling rather like molting snakes. We dined on vichyssoise, cold crab meat and brandied peaches. The boy refused to sleep in the house saying simply that it was "very bad place." So we dragged a mattress to the garage and slept there the carbines ready a snub-nosed thirty-eight by each hand. Never keep a pistol under your pillow where you have to reach up for it. Keep it down by your hand at the crotch. That way you can come up shooting right through the blanket.

At dawn we set out through the ruined suburbs no signs of life the air windless and dead. From time to time the boy would stop sniffing like a dog. "This way Meester." We were walking down a long avenue littered with palm branches. Suddenly the air was full of robins thousands of them settling in the ruined gardens perching on the empty houses splashing in bird baths full of rain water. A boy on a red bicycle flashed past. He made a wide U-turn and pulled in to the curb beside us. He was naked except for a red jockstrap, belt and flexible black shoes his flesh red as terra cotta smooth poreless skin tight over the cheekbones deep-set black eyes and a casque of black hair. At his belt was an eighteen-inch bowie knife with knuckle-duster handle. He said no word of greeting. He sat there one foot on the curb looking at the Dib. His ears which stuck out from the head trembled slightly and his eyes glistened. He licked his lips and said one word in a language unknown to me. The Dib nodded matter of factly. He turned to me. "He very hot. Been riding three days. Fuck now talk later."

The boy propped his bicycle against the curb. He took off his belt and knife and dropped them on a bench. He sat down on the bench and shoved his jockstrap down

over his shoes. His red cock flipped out stiff and lubricating. The boy stood up. Beneath thin red ribs his
heart throbbed and pounded. The Dib peeled off his
jockstrap scraping erection. He stepped out of the strap
and tossed the boy a tin of Vaseline from his shoeshine
box. The boy caught it and rubbed Vaseline on his cock
throbbing to his heartbeats. The Dib stepped toward
him and the boy caught him by the hips turning him
around. The Dib parted his cheeks with both hands
leaning forward and the red penis quivered into his
flesh. Holding the Dib's hips in both hands the boy's
body contracted pulling together. His ears began to
vibrate lips parted from long yellow teeth smooth and
hard as old ivory. His deep-set black eyes lit up inside
with red fire and the hair stood up straight on his head.
The Dib's body arched spurting pearly gobs in the
stagnant sunlight. For a few seconds they shivered together then the boy shoved the Dib's body away as if
he were taking off a garment. They went to a pool
across a lawn washed themselves came back and put on
their jockstraps.
"This Jimmy the Shrew. He messenger special delivery
C.O.D." They talked briefly in their language which is
transliterated from a picture language known to all wild
boys in this area.
"He say time barrier ahead. Very bad."
The Shrew took a small flat box from his handle-bar
basket and handed it to the Dib. "He giving us film
grenades." The Dib opened the box and showed me six
small black cylinders. The Shrew got on his bicycle and
rode away down the avenue and disappeared in a
blaze of hibiscus. We walked on through the suburbs
heading north. The houses were smaller and shabbier.
A menace and evil hung in the empty streets like a haze

and the air was getting cold around the edges. We rounded a corner and a sharp wind spattered the Dib's body with goose pimples. He sniffed uneasily.

"We coming to bad place, Johnny. Need clothes."

"Let's see what we can find in here."

There was a rambling ranch-style house obviously built before the naborhood had deteriorated. We stepped through a hedge and passed a ruined barbecue pit. The side door was open. We were in a room that had served as an office. In a drawer of the desk the Dib found a thirty-eight snub-nosed revolver and box of shells.

"Whee look" he cried and popped his find into the shoe-shine box. We went through the house like a whirlwind the Dib pulling out suits and sports coats from closets and holding them against his body in front of mirrors, opening drawers snatching what he wanted and dumping the rest on the floor. His eyes shone and his excitement mounted as we rushed from room to room throwing any clothes we might use onto beds and chairs and sofas. I felt a wet-dream tension in my crotch the dream of packing to leave with a few minutes to catch a boat and more and more drawers full of clothes to pack the boat whistling in the harbor. As we stepped into a little guest room the Dib in front of me I stroked his smooth white buttocks and he turned to me rubbing his jock.

"This make me very hot Meester." He sat down on the bed and pulled off his jockstrap and his cock flipped out lubricating. "Whee" he said and lay back on his elbows kicking his feet. "Jacking me off." I slipped off my strap and sat down beside him rubbing the lubricant around the tip of his cock and he went off in a few seconds.

We took a shower and made a selection of clothes or rather I made the selection since the Dib's taste ran to loud sports coats wide ties and straw hats. I found a blue suit for him and he looked like a 1920 prep school boy on vacation. For myself I selected a grey Glen Plaid and a green fedora. We packed the spare gun and extra shells into a brief case with the film grenades the Shrew had given us.

Fish smells and dead eyes in doorways shabby quarters of a forgotten city streets half-buried in sand. I was beginning to remember the pawn shops, guns and brass knucks in a dusty window, cheap rooming houses, chili parlors, a cold wind from the sea. Police line ahead frisking seven boys against a wall. Too late to turn back they'd seen us. And then I saw the photographers, more photographers than a routine frisk would draw. I eased a film grenade into my hand. A cop stopped toward us. I pushed the plunger down and brought my hands up tossing the grenade into the air. A black explosion blotted out the set and we were running down a dark street toward the barrier. We ran on and burst out of a black silver mist into late afternoon sunlight on a suburban street, cracked pavements, sharp smell of weeds.

THE PENNY ARCADE PEEP SHOW

Naked boys standing by a water hole savanna backdrop a head of giraffe in the distance. The boys talk in growls and snarls, purrs and yipes and show their teeth at each other like wild dogs. Two boys fuck standing up squeezing back teeth bare, hair stands up on the ankles, ripples up the legs in goose pimples they whine and whimper off.

In the rotten flesh gardens languid Bubu boys with black smiles scratch erogenous sores diseased putrid sweet their naked bodies steam of a sepia haze of nitrous choking vapors.

Green lizard boy by a stagnant stream smiles and rubs

his worn leather jockstrap with one slow finger.

Dim street light on soiled clothes boy stands there naked with his shirt in one hand the other hand scratching his ass.

Two naked youths with curly black hair and pointed Pan ears casting dice by a marble fountain. The loser bends over looking at his reflection in the pool. The winner poises behind him like a phallic god. He pries the smooth white buttocks apart with his thumbs. Lips curl back from sharp white teeth. Laughter shakes the sky.

Glider boys drift down from the sunset on red wings and rain arrows from the sky.

Slingshot boys glide in across a valley riding their black plastic wings like sheets of mica in the sunlight torn clothes flapping hard red flesh. Each boy carries a heavy slingshot attached to his wrist by a leather thong. At their belts are leather pouches of round black stones.

The roller-skate boys sweep down a hill in a shower of autumn leaves. They slice through a police patrol. Blood spatters dead leaves in air.

The screen is exploding in moon craters and boiling silver spots.

"Wild boys very close now."

Darkness falls on the ruined suburbs. A dog barks in the distance.

Dim jerky stars are blowing away across a gleaming empty sky, *the wild boys smile.*

William S. Burroughs
August 17, 1969
London